Also by Natasha D. Frazier

Editor: Chandra Sparks Splond

For autographed copies, please visit:
www.natashafrazier.com

Acknowledgements

With God's grace, I've done it again. There is something amazing about filling a blank word document with 54,000 words. And with every published book, I get a little more excited. This is now my new favorite story and I hope it'll become yours, too.

None of this would be possible if my Heavenly Father didn't give me the capacity and provision to do the thing that I love—write. So, thank You, Lord.

My husband, Eddie, and my children Eden, Ethan, and Emilyn—thank you for your love and support. I couldn't do this without my family's support.

My sister, Amber—Thank you for stepping in to help out with my children when needed and often without being asked.

Chandra—Thank you for your editing expertise. This story wouldn't be as amazing without you.

Special thank you to my sisters, Tiera, Toccara, and Shenitra, who have prayed with me and encouraged me in my journey.

Page 35, you guys consistently strengthen me as a writer. I'm grateful to have each of you in my corner. Thank you.

Mom and Dad—I wouldn't be here if it weren't for you. Thank you for encouraging me to "go for the trophy."

And the Dream Team—Your ears are probably fried by now, yet, you continue to listen and help me brainstorm. Teamwork certainly makes the dream work. Thank you for being part of my team.

Dearest reader—Thank you for supporting me by reading, reviewing, and sharing my books with others. (Please don't stop.) You're all I think about as I write. Enjoy Ava and Zack's journey to each other through all the turmoil.

Natasha

THE WRONG SEAT

Langston Sisters Series Book 2

Chapter One

In a few months, Langston Brands could be a luxury handbag business of the past.

At least that's the way Ava Langston saw it. Special thanks to her oldest sister's murder charges. Although the charges were dismissed against their chief executive officer Crystal Langston six months ago, their family's business hadn't bounced back from the negative attention the way they'd hoped. Sales were down twenty percent, and the launch of their newest collection was an epic fail.

But tonight was an opportunity for Ava to lock in the largest deal Langston Brands had secured since its inception back in 1952. It wouldn't hurt to be the family's savior this go-round and receive her due praise. Even at thirty-nine years old, she sometimes suffered from middle-child syndrome—struggling to find where she fit in and to prove her worth.

Ava shimmied her shoulders, shaking off the dark thoughts, and continued her navigation toward her destination. She'd work hard for her family's business, regardless of their gratitude, just as she'd done for the last eighteen years.

Her phone rang through her car's Bluetooth speakers. Ava rolled her eyes at the name displayed on dashboard's LCD screen: Rick Fuller. She'd swear he forgot he was no longer acting CEO.

"Please tell me you're on time to meet the buyer. I don't have to tell you how much we need this."

Ava twisted her face in a scowl she wished Rick could see. Punctuality had never been an issue of hers. She'd expect a call like that from her father, Lamont Langston, or even from Crystal, or her younger sister, Layla, who was vice president of public relations at their family-owned company.

"I am. In fact, I'm early." Ava didn't have time to indulge him. She was minutes from arriving at her scheduled dinner at Taste of Houston with the buyer. Maybe she had Rick to thank for the meeting. The buyer was married to one of his cousins, which is how they'd received the first contract a couple of years ago. She softened her tone. "Is there anything else you need?"

"Just making sure everything is on schedule. We don't want any hiccups."

One would think he owned the company.

"Don't worry, Rick. I've got this. I'm meeting with Crystal first thing in the morning. I assume you'll be there, too."

"Indeed, I will."

Ava ended the call with Rick, cut her engine, grabbed her purse, and stepped out into the March breeze. Cool temperatures in March were rare, but she welcomed the fall-like weather. With about ten minutes to spare, she shuffled into the restaurant and gave her name to the hostess. The buyer, Ms. Wertheimer, hadn't arrived yet.

The hostess escorted Ava to their reserved table tucked away in a corner. Cozy, Ava removed her light pea coat and scoped her surroundings.

The patrons appeared to be couples completely engrossed in each other and their steak dinners. One man who sat alone seemed like he was waiting for someone to join him. From time to time, she caught him staring at her. Any other time, she'd consider it a compliment, but not after what happened to her sister Crystal who had been kidnapped in the middle of the day, forced to ride with her kidnapper, and held at gunpoint. That incident made Ava suspicious of most strangers.

Crystal's kidnapping happened six months ago, but Ava couldn't lie and say the situation didn't leave her on edge. What were the odds of that happening to her or Layla, too? Slim, but obviously one could never be too careful.

The stranger across the room dressed in a black suit was what she considered a muscle man. Buff. Probably would do well as a bodyguard. It wouldn't surprise her if he touched a device in his ear and started talking to a team to alert them he had eyes on his target.

Ava chuckled and picked up the menu.

Too many crime drama movies.

And too much going on in her family.

Thankfully, her guest arrived to stave off any additional runaway thoughts about potential criminals.

"Miss Langston, so good to see you again." At about five feet five inches, Ms. Wertheimer stood shoulder to shoulder with Ava. She smelled as expensive as she looked with her short chin-length haircut, a strand of pearls adorning her neck, and a navy designer dress with a matching handbag.

"Please call me Ava." Every time they met—about three times a year for the past four years—Ava encouraged the woman to address her by her first name. She never did.

"If you'll call me Lisa." Ms. Wertheimer's southern twang reminded Ava of one of *The Golden Girls* actors. Though married into Rick Fuller's family, Ms. Wertheimer kept her family's last name.

Ava offered a smile, but her eyes drifted back in the direction of the handsome bodyguard-looking man. She could feel his eyes on her. He'd been looking at her as if they knew each other, hadn't he? That notion could be all in her head.

She met and mingled with different people all the time. She'd remember if she'd met that man prior to tonight.

Ava sipped her glass of water and did her best to dismiss him and focus on Ms. Wertheimer.

"So, what is this big news?"

Ms. Wertheimer tapped her red manicured nails on the table. "We signed a deal to buy out Fitzgerald, which means we'll own the largest department store in the world."

"That is amazing. Congratulations."

"I came here to discuss partnering with Langston Brands to sell your bags in our stores."

Ava could have sworn her body went numb. She couldn't wait to share this news with the board of directors. Since sales in their own stores had dropped consistently over the past few months, maybe a new partnership would do them some good, especially with a designer retail partner like Wertheimer, who'd just bought out Fitzgerald. The added Fitzgerald stores would double their sales potential. In her mind, this new partnership was a done deal.

"However…"

Ava's belly kissed her feet at Ms. Wertheimer's tone. She leaned forward and braced her fingers on the table. *Give it to me straight.*

"There've been accusations circulating about Langston Brands' manufacturing practices since you moved some production offshore two years ago."

"Such as?"

Ms. Wertheimer's eyes grew wider, and she tilted her head to the side. Was she trying to get a message across without saying it? Because Ava didn't understand. The waitress returned and took their orders. Ava's appetite withered, but she ordered a six-ounce steak with steamed broccoli anyway.

When the waitress left their table, Ms. Wertheimer said, "There are allegations that Langston Brands is operating a sweatshop in Cambodia. Low wages, poor working conditions, and underage workers."

"That's insane. You know that isn't true," Ava half-whined. She had to stop and catch herself. She wasn't a child in trouble. She was an adult who had a serious issue to deal with—an issue that had the likelihood of destroying her family's brand. Suddenly, Ava got the urge to slip back into her coat as goosebumps popped up along her bare arms.

Lord, why is this happening?

Was Crystal's situation not enough tribulation?

Ms. Wertheimer looked doubtful, like she had information Ava wasn't privy to.

"I suggest you investigate it. These allegations will need to be cleared before we can finalize any new partnerships with Langston Brands."

Ava leaned back in her seat, shoulders slumped, and searched her memory for anything in the past that could lead her to believe there was any truth to what Ms. Wertheimer had just revealed.

How could anything like that be happening and her family not know about it?

Or worse. Could it be true and someone in her family did know what was going on?

"I'll find out why these allegations have come about, but I can assure you Langston Brands takes pride in labor relations and how we treat all employees."

Ms. Wertheimer nodded. "Good. Keep me posted on what you find out and actions your company intends to take to rectify the situation."

Rectify the situation? Was Ms. Wertheimer convinced the allegations were true?

Ava forced herself to sit through dinner once their entrees arrived. The sweatshop allegations dominated her thoughts. In her mind, there wasn't much more that could be said. This could ruin them.

After dinner ended, they bid their goodbyes. Once outside of the restaurant, Ava whipped her phone out to call her sisters on conference call. This sweatshop issue wasn't something that could wait for a morning meeting discussion.

"Ava, is that you?"

Ava swiveled her head in the direction of the familiar voice. "Aunt Elaine, hi. How've you been?" Though she adored Elaine Waters, a woman who was like family to the Langstons and worked at their company for more than twenty years, Ava forced a smile. She hadn't talked to her in the five years since Elaine had left Langston Brands. The polite thing to do would be to spend a few minutes talking to her or at least promise to call, but thoughts of a potential sweatshop operation taunted her.

Elaine wrapped her arms around Ava's neck. "I've been well. It's so good to see you." She pulled away and held Ava at arm's length. "You look amazing."

Ava felt her smile become more genuine. "Thank you."

"I'm meeting a friend for dinner, but let's catch up soon. It's been too long."

"I agree. Let's schedule lunch sometime."

"I look forward to it." Elaine kissed her cheek and vanished as quickly as she'd appeared.

Ava made a mental note to contact Elaine later while she dealt with the situation that was minutes from making her lose her mind. First, she called Crystal, then asked her to add Layla to the call. When she arrived at her car, a tissue was tucked in the door handle.

Ewww.

She grabbed the tissue by her fingernails and threw it to the ground.

"We've got a problem," Ava said when both of her sisters were on the line. She reached for the door handle, but her hand fell limp at her side. In a matter of seconds, her body grew weak, and everything went dark.

∞

Zack Kingsland arrived at Taste of Houston five minutes before Ava Langston. His only job that evening was to surveil Ava. After all, he wasn't certain if this was a job his private security firm, The Four Kings, should take on. When he spoke to Lamont Langston a week ago, the man offered to pay whatever fee they asked if The Four Kings would keep an eye on his three daughters. What bothered Zack was that Lamont didn't offer any solid reasoning of why they needed protection. But Zack's brother,

Ezekiel, encouraged him to take the contract. Good for business, he said. This contract would keep their people working and would be less dangerous than some of their other work. And it was an opportunity for Zack to get back in the field. The youngest brothers, twins Jacob and Joshua, agreed with Zeke, as they affectionately referred to Ezekiel.

As the person least interested in the gig, somehow Zack ended up being the one tasked with keeping an eye on the middle sister, Ava. Lamont passed on her calendar of meetings, and Zack attended each one, at a distance of course. But tonight, that wasn't possible.

Tonight was the first time he'd ever gotten as close as he did. Close enough to notice how beautiful the woman was. Caramel skin that reminded him of what he'd find inside of a candy bar. A dentist-approved smile. A cute perky nose. And eyes that almost made him forget his mission. Even her short hair shone in the dim restaurant lighting. There was a time or two tonight she caught him staring at her—something he prided himself on never doing, yet he couldn't help himself.

There was nothing about her that would make him think someone would want to harm her. She didn't meet with any dangerous people. Her schedule was boring. Coffee shop on the way into the office. Lunch meetings at upscale Houston restaurants. Fitness classes before or after work.

And tonight's dinner with an older woman was as boring as could be. He listened but didn't pick up anything in her conversation that would warrant a need for a bodyguard or private security firm to be involved. Her family owned a handbag business. Why would someone want to harm her? To steal as many handbags as possible and sell them for personal gain?

That was insane just to think about.

When he was a detective on the police force, he worked more exciting cases, but that part of his life was over, and he never wanted to go back.

Tomorrow, he'd call Lamont Langston and demand answers. He needed more information if the man wanted him to keep this up. From what he'd learned about Ava, there was no reason to continue. If his brothers liked the idea so much, one of them could take this on, but he was out.

He sent a message to their group text.

I'm positive there's better work than this. Who's got next on this case? I think I'm done.

Zack waited a couple of minutes for Ava to leave the restaurant. When she cleared the doorway, he left a tip on the table for his own steak dinner and vacated the area. Zack stepped outside of the restaurant and eyed Ava across the parking lot at her car door. From a distance, she appeared wobbly. He didn't see her drinking, so his interest piqued, and his internal alarm went off. Ava tumbled to the ground.

Maybe he'd been wrong and his instincts about this case were off. Zack sprinted across the parking lot. He darted his eyes around the area to see if he noted anything or anyone suspicious.

Nothing.

In twenty seconds, maybe less, Zack made it to her car and knelt at her side.

"Ava, Ava. Can you hear me?" Zack pressed two fingers to the side of her neck. She was still breathing, but her breath was shallow.

He didn't think she had enough time for him to call for an ambulance, wait for them to arrive, then take her to a hospital.

Zack spotted her phone on the ground, a call in progress.

"I'm taking Ava to the hospital. She was passed out on the ground in the parking lot outside the Taste of Houston," Zack said to the caller without introducing himself.

"Who is this?" called one woman.

"What happened? What hospital?" another woman's voice said.

"I'm Zack Kingsland. Memorial Hermann is right up the road on Gessner. Meet me there," Zack said and ended the call. He could only assume the women on the line were the other Langston sisters.

He wasn't parked far away from her, so he picked up her limp body. Though she couldn't weigh any more than one hundred forty pounds, it felt like she had an extra thirty pounds added to her weight.

Zack took quick, determined strides to his vehicle. He secured her in the back seat of his 4x4 and then climbed behind the wheel. In three minutes, Zack arrived at the emergency room entrance and threw his gear into park. He jogged around the cab to open the door and pulled Ava from the back seat.

Cupping her in his arms, he charged through the automatic doors. "She needs help—now."

An emergency room nurse ran to his aid, followed by another with a gurney.

"What's her name? What happened?" the nurse called out.

"Ava Langston." Zack lowered her onto the gurney. "I don't know what happened to her. She was already passed out when I found her in a restaurant parking lot a few minutes away."

The nurse shoved the earpiece of her stethoscope into her ears and pressed the chest piece in several places across Ava's chest, then shouted a request for CCs of some medicine in medical terms he didn't recognize. They wheeled Ava away and began their work to help her regain consciousness.

Zack released a heavy breath as he watched them take her further into the emergency department. That was a strange change of events. Now he had to wonder if she was somehow poisoned and whether that incident had to do with the reason her father hired his private security firm.

Zack called his brother Zeke to fill him in on what happened with Ava. Less than an hour ago, he was ready to pass on this job— or at least hand it off to one of his brothers—but now he was curious enough to dig a little deeper to see if this situation was coincidental or intentional. His call with Zeke lasted about ten minutes. When two women stormed into the emergency room, almost identical to Ava, he ended the call.

"You must be Crystal and Layla," he said.

"Yes. Are you Zack?" one of them answered. "I'm Layla, Ava's sister. What happened to her?"

"I'm not sure. Hopefully the medical team can give us more answers when they're done with their tests. I found her collapsed on the ground in the parking lot near her car."

Crystal inhaled sharply, and her eyes looked like they were about to jump out of their sockets. She eyed her sister Layla.

"And just who are you? And why were you there? How do we know you didn't do anything to her?" Layla questioned.

Zack wasn't sure how much their father had told them or if he'd shared anything with them about hiring a private security firm to look after them, but primarily Ava, since she traveled out of the country most often. But he wasn't about to be accused of anything.

"Ask your father about The Four Kings. He knows who I am."

Layla didn't waste a second. She whipped her phone from her back pocket and called her father. She kept her eyes on him while she engaged her father in her own interrogation. When she ended the call, she pursed her lips and maintained a suspicious eye. "*Umph,*" she uttered.

"Well, what did he say?" Crystal shoved an elbow into Layla's side.

13

"Not much. Only that he can vouch for him, and he's legit. He said he'll explain everything when he gets here."

What in the world had Lamont Langston and the Kingsland brothers gotten him into? He should step away while he still had the good sense to do so, but curiosity was getting the best of him. And he never walked away from an unsolved case.

Looks like he'd have to rescind everything he'd said to Zeke earlier that evening. He wouldn't walk away from this gig. Not yet. Not until he determined if this was just a one-off incident or whether someone really wanted Ava gone.

And if so, why?

Either way, it finally looked like this was a case worth pursuing.

Chapter Two

*Z*ack hung around the emergency room to speak with Lamont Langston face-to-face. Now was a good time for the old man to come clean and enlighten Zack about what they were truly up against. He wasn't one to take on a security contract just because there was a high-dollar value attached to it. But then again, he'd practically shielded himself from any work that meant he had to deal with their clients directly. His brother Zeke accepted the job with Lamont on behalf of The Four Kings. It was past time for Zack to find out what Zeke had gotten him into and why Lamont wanted the brothers personally involved instead of one of their employees.

Lamont trotted into the emergency room looking like he'd just left an important business meeting, dressed in a tailored black three-piece suit with shoes shinier than a kid lathered in petroleum jelly. His wife, Dana, skirted in front of him. Zack watched the two embrace Crystal and Layla. After hugging, the family remained in one another's personal space.

Zack nodded a greeting to Lamont when he looked away from his family and locked eyes with him. Zack hadn't met him, but

Zeke had. And he'd heard his entire life how much he and his brothers looked like each other—spitting images of their late father, folks would say. So Lamont had to know who he was and why he was there, despite never having been formally introduced. He excused himself from his family and strolled over to Zack with an outstretched hand.

"Lamont Langston. You're Zack Kingsland. Am I right?"

Zack crossed his arms over his chest. "You are."

"Thank you for saving my daughter and bringing her here tonight. I know I made the right decision when I hired The Four Kings."

A worried expression flashed across Lamont's face.

"I'm glad you mentioned that. I can't be effective if I don't know why I'm hired or what I'm looking for."

Lamont looked over his shoulder and eyed his family for a few seconds, then turned his attention back to Zack. He led them to a sitting area farther away from his family.

"I understand." Lamont cleared his throat. "Like I shared with your brother Ezekiel when I first reached out to him, I wasn't quite sure how much I needed your help. This was more of a precaution. But now I see I made the right call."

Zack nodded and waited for him to continue. Lamont still hadn't given him the information he was looking for. Something concrete. A cause for real concern. A reason to believe Ava was targeted tonight.

Lamont looked over his shoulder again before he continued speaking.

"For the last three weeks, rumors have been circulating about our company running sweatshops in Cambodia. Of course, there isn't any merit to these accusations. What concerns me is the veiled threats and warnings I've received."

"What kind of threats—phone calls? Notes? Emails?"

"Letters without a return address in my office mail."

"Do you still have them?"

Lamont nodded and slipped his hand inside of his suit jacket to retrieve his phone. "I haven't shared these with anyone just yet, but here are pictures of the letters." He passed his phone to Zack and darted his eyes in the direction of his wife and daughters.

If I lose my investment in Langston Brands because of your unethical business practices, plan to lose your daughters, too.

Handle the situation ASAP. The more I lose, the more you'll lose.

Have you checked today's stock prices? If you don't care about your stock being worthless, I guess your family is worthless to you, too. Shall we start with Ava?

Zack's heart slammed in his chest.

At least the last letter answered his question. Ava was indeed targeted. And since he already started the job, he was committed to finishing it. He wouldn't stop until this person was caught before they caused more harm to the woman.

Zack turned the phone toward Lamont with the screen highlighting the letter that named Ava. "Is this one the most recent?"

"Yes."

"Do you have any idea who could be behind the letters?"

"From the tone of the messages, it could be a stockholder, which could be anyone."

"My team can take it from here, but we need full cooperation and transparency, which means you need to tell your family what's happening. We'll deploy resources for Crystal and Layla. I'll cover Ava, so it's important that she's aware of what's happening and for her to know that I'll be her personal bodyguard until this situation gets resolved."

What would Ava think about this arrangement?

For Zack, it was the only alternative.

No one else would die on his watch.

Ever again.

"I understand."

"Lamont, I know this environment isn't ideal, but Ava's life is at stake, so this conversation needs to happen now. Call them over, and when the doctor gives the okay for you to see Ava, you'll need to talk with her, too."

Under normal circumstances, Zack would have given Lamont more time to talk to his family away from the hospital, but Lamont's daughter was lying in a hospital bed because someone had already attempted to harm her. This wouldn't become another situation he'd shoulder the blame for because he didn't act on instinct. He vowed not to lose another life.

Who's to say how far this person would go and when their next attempt to harm Ava would be? They'd already proven they were serious. There wasn't much time to waste. And Zack was certain Crystal and Layla had questions about who he was and why he was still there, especially given the fact that Lamont spent the last ten minutes talking to him.

Crystal and Layla glared at him several times, giving him the proverbial evil eye. Did they believe he had something to do with Ava winding up in the hospital? He couldn't be sure, but their eyes screamed mistrust.

"I can step away and give you some time if you'd like," Zack offered, crouching on the edge of his seat.

"No, no, that's not necessary. There's no time like the present for us all to be acquainted." Lamont waved his wife and daughters over to where he and Zack sat.

Layla looked between the two of them. "What's going on, Dad?" She squinted at Zack, as if he was the cause of her pain.

Dana sat next to him and took hold of his hand.

Lamont gestured toward Zack. "This is Zack Kingsland from The Four Kings, a private security company I hired."

"For what?" Layla's outburst rang throughout the area, causing stares from the emergency room staff. Her face was contorted in a frown, and she'd tossed her hands in the air quick enough for him to feel a gust of air following the movement.

19

Dana's mouth hung open, and her eyes widened. She crooked her head to the side, obviously not pleased with being left out.

Crystal shook her head and clutched her collarbone. The fear was evident in her horror-stricken eyes. "Are you kidding me? Tell me this isn't happening again."

Zack was familiar with Crystal and the news of her being accused of murdering her ex-husband, but this situation had nothing to do with that.

Lamont gave them a stern look, probably one he'd given to them as children as a warning to be quiet. "The sweatshop rumors seem to have gotten someone stirred up." Lamont told them about the letters, just as he'd shared the information with Zack. "And I think this person could be behind what happened to Ava. Zack is here to protect her. Both of you have protection details as well. I can't risk anything happening to either of you."

"And at this point, we have to take every threat seriously," Zack added. "Have either of you noticed anything suspicious lately?"

Crystal squinted as if she was thinking through past events. "No, I haven't."

"Me either," Layla added.

Zack pulled out his phone and showed them photos of his brothers. "These are my twin brothers. They've been surveilling you. We'll set up a meeting so you all can meet the team and everyone is in the loop. It works best that way. We're going to keep you all safe and do our best to solve this case as soon as possible."

"Dad, you had us followed and didn't tell us?" Layla exploded and shoved her fists into her hips. She cocked her head to the side, and Zack almost expected her to tap her foot in expectation of getting her questions answered.

"It's for your own good. We can talk more about it later if you wish, but in the meantime, your safety is what's more important to me."

Layla's frown softened a little. Zack sensed she had more questions, but she didn't say anything more. Lamont turned his attention to Zack and extended his hand again. "Thanks, Zack. I appreciate everything The Four Kings will do to help us get this settled."

Zack gripped Lamont's hand in a firm shake. "You're welcome."

Was Lamont attempting to dismiss him?

Had he not made himself clear?

Zack settled back in his seat and crossed his ankle over his knee. "I'll stick around to keep an eye on Ava. When the doctor gives the okay for you to see her, I will be there."

∞

Ava struggled to part her heavy eyelids.

Beeping machines were her only companions. An intravenous needle was inserted into her right arm, pumping fluid.

Her memory was a fog as she fought to recall how she wound up in a hospital bed.

She had dinner with Ms. Wertheimer and remembered walking back to her car. She'd been determined to talk to her sisters about the sweatshop accusations. Then there was the strangest thing—a tissue tucked in her door handle.

A nurse entered the room sporting a pair of green scrubs and a smile. Her curly tendrils were pulled back in a ponytail. "You pulled through. You had us worried here for a minute," the young woman said. The nurse checked Ava's vitals and switched out the near-empty bag hanging on the poll. Though she smiled, Ava sensed something was still terribly wrong. "I'll send the doctor right in," she announced on her way out of the room.

Minutes later, a doctor with the height and body mass of an NBA player who played center position entered the room. Ava shifted in the hospital bed to sit comfortably upright.

"Good evening, Miss Langston. I'm Dr. Pemberton."

"Good evening. What happened to me? The last thing I remember is leaving the restaurant and walking to my car."

Dr. Pemberton posed with his hands crossed in front of him, the electronic tablet in one hand. "What did you have for dinner?"

"Steak and steamed broccoli."

Dr. Pemberton slid his fingers over the electronic tablet's screen. His eyebrows furrowed, but what troubled Ava more was his silence.

"What's wrong? Was it the food I ate? Did I get food poisoning or something?"

"We've run a few blood tests and found rat poison in your system. We also identified a second poisonous substance, which may have entered your body by something you touched."

Ava sucked in a stream of air and glanced down at her right hand—the hand she used to pluck the tissue away from her door handle. She recounted the story to the doctor.

"I think that'll explain how the unidentified substance entered your system. We've treated you for both, and your body has responded well to the treatments, but we'll keep you overnight for observation. Your family is in the waiting room. I'll send them in."

"Thanks, Dr. Pemberton."

Layla and Crystal rushed to her bedside, each of them taking turns squeezing her in their arms. When they pulled away, her mother and father repeated the gesture.

"I'm so glad you're alright. This was scary," Layla said.

Ava's stomach weaved into tiny knots. Scary was an understatement. "The doctor said I was poisoned. That restaurant is supposed to be one of the best. How could something like that happen? I'm filing a lawsuit."

Layla, Crystal, and their mom looked to Lamont.

And Ava wasn't sure why, but beads of sweat formed along her hairline. Crystal wore that same look when she tried to hide what was happening after Dante's murder. She had a terrible poker face. For sure Ava thought Layla would be ready to back her up in this, yet her lips were sealed. That was a miracle if she'd ever witnessed one. She wasn't quite sure what her mom thought about the idea of her suing the local restaurant because she was the very definition of demure. She despised confrontation and usually left it up to their father to take care of things. So it wasn't unusual to see her deferring to him, yet it bothered Ava. It was the look in her mom's eyes, like all of them had a secret.

Her dad slid a seat next to her bed, sat, and cupped one of her hands in both of his.

Lamont kissed the back of her hand.

"I'm so glad you're okay."

"Me, too. Dad, what's wrong?"

"Rumors have been circulating about our company operating sweatshops in our manufacturing facilities in Cambodia."

"Ms. Wertheimer mentioned that. I assured her that isn't true."

"Right, but to help put the rumors to rest, I'm going to visit our facilities in Cambodia and Vietnam."

"Okay. Sounds like a good plan, but I take it that's not all you want to tell me."

"I don't believe you being poisoned is an accident. I've received threats telling me to do something about the sweatshop accusations, and if I didn't, this person will come after my daughters, starting with you."

"Dad, why didn't you tell me?" Ava shrieked, causing several coughs to follow.

"I didn't want to alarm you, but I have taken steps to keep you safe."

"How's that?"

Lamont rose from his seat and glided toward the door. He poked his head outside and stepped back inside the room with the man from the restaurant.

"I know him," Ava said as the man followed her father into the room. He was even more handsome up close. She pointed at him. "I saw you at the restaurant tonight."

The man extended his hand toward her, swallowing her hand in his. "I'm Zack Kingsland."

An unfamiliar warmth engulfed the entire right side of her body. When he released her, the warmth was replaced with goosebumps and an emptiness she couldn't explain. Ava linked her fingers and rested them in her lap.

"Zack is the one who found you collapsed in the parking lot tonight. If it weren't for his quick thinking, you may not be here with us right now."

"How do we know he isn't responsible for what happened to me?" Before the words left her lips, instinct told her he wasn't responsible, but she couldn't immediately discount him after everything Crystal had gone through.

Zack crooked his head to the side and eyed her. She'd go so far as to say that he silently challenged her accusation. There was a certain warmth in his gaze that made her want to look longer into his chestnut eyes, but if she kept it up, things might've gotten weird.

25

"Because I've hired him as your personal bodyguard. Zack is part owner of the private security firm The Four Kings. When I wasn't sure how serious the threats were, his only job was to watch you from a distance, but now you can expect him to be a lot closer."

"And how is that supposed to work exactly? I can't have a bodyguard. I have a job to do. Don't you think that'll bring about more questions if he's following me around everywhere?"

"Miss Langston, we can work out the details to your comfort level, but you need me, especially since someone is out to hurt you. And I'll be around until we figure out who it is and put them in police custody."

"What if I want to go on a date?"

"Like I said, we can make arrangements—"

Layla blurted out, "Girl, please. When is the last time you went on a date?"

Their mom swatted Layla's shoulder. "Stop it. This is a serious matter."

Crystal covered her mouth and hid her laugh behind her hand.

Ava frowned and looked from Layla to Zack, as if to remind her they had company present. If Ava had invisibility superpowers, now would've been the time to use them, although she wasn't surprised at Layla's outburst. She was the only person in their family who usually spoke her mind.

"I'm not here to disrupt your personal life, only to ensure your safety, Miss Langston."

"And just how can you ensure my safety? What are your qualifications?" Sure, her dad probably knew about his background, but to her, he was still a handsome stranger.

Lamont poised himself to speak, but Zack held up his hand and stopped him.

"I served as a police officer in the Houston Police Department for fifteen years and have been in private security with my brothers for the last five years."

"Why'd you leave HPD?"

Ava saw what she could only assume to be pain flash in his eyes. He had to expect that question, but the way he responded told her he didn't. "Personal reasons. Private security is more suitable for me."

Ava nodded. Now she was even more curious.

"Is there anything else I can answer for you, Miss Langston?"

He held her gaze for a moment, but then looked pointedly at everyone else in the room who shook their heads and said, "No."

"Not at this time."

"Okay, Miss Langston. Although I was at the restaurant tonight, I need to talk to you about your conversation with the woman you were with and what happened when you left. Are you up for it?"

"Yes."

He pulled a chair up to her bedside, but her dad interrupted. "You can have my seat. We'll get out of your way so you two can work together. The sooner we can get this handled, the better."

Her family said their good-byes with promises to call and come by tomorrow morning.

When they left the room, Ava took a deep breath and said, "Alright, I'm ready, but you have to do me a favor."

"What's that?"

"Please call me Ava."

The corners of his lips finally turned upward, and Ava spotted a dimple. Smooth bald head. Caramel skin. Neatly shaven goatee. Soul-stirring eyes. A baritone voice she was certain she'd hear in her dreams. Great. Physically, he checked all her boxes, but it sucked that she couldn't explore more because he'd just been hired as her babysitter.

Life was grand.

Chapter Three

Zack and his three brothers started The Four Kings private security firm five years ago, so this wouldn't be the first time he'd worked in the capacity of a personal bodyguard. He'd also done a few private security details while employed by the Houston Police Department. And though he'd committed to protecting Ava, he wasn't sure why he didn't feel settled about the ordeal.

He positioned himself near her bedside in the seat Lamont vacated and rested his elbows on his thighs. Even after a week of surveilling Ava, he wasn't prepared to be near her. When they shook hands a moment ago, something transpired between them unlike anything he'd ever felt. And he'd been married before, so he knew about chemistry, love, and connection. But her touch was different, a combination of him wanting to hold her hand to see if he'd feel the strange feeling twice and the urge to never do so again.

Ava's eyes captured his. Zack nodded without breaking eye contact. "Okay. Start from the beginning."

Ava scrunched her eyebrows and looked at him like he'd grown another pair of eyes. "You don't think Ms. Wertheimer has anything to do with poisoning me, do you?"

"I don't have any thoughts yet. Let's start with the purpose of your meeting and what you discussed."

"Ms. Wertheimer is a buyer who Langston Brands has worked with in the past. We tend to meet a few times a year, and tonight was one of those meetings. She expressed interest in placement of our handbags in their new stores. Her family owns Wertheimer and just recently bought out Fitzgerald, so basically it would be an expanded distribution type of deal."

"Did she seem aggressive? Was anything about her behavior tonight different from other times you've met with her?"

"No, not really. The only strange thing she mentioned was the accusation of Langston Brands operating sweatshops in our manufacturing facilities outside the U.S. I'd think that would be a concern with any buyer."

Zack squinted and thought for a moment about the information he had so far. Someone was clearly targeting Ava because of the sweatshop allegations. This person had to have been at the restaurant tonight—or possibly paid someone to do their dirty work for them. And this person was also highly likely a Langston Brands shareholder.

"Okay. Now tell me what happened when you walked out of the restaurant back to your car. Did you notice anyone in the area or hear anything?"

"I did not, but I was overly focused on calling my sisters to talk about the conversation I'd had with Ms. Wertheimer. Someone could have been in the area, but I probably wouldn't have noticed." Ava told him about the wadded-up tissue paper tucked in her door handle and the discussion she had with her doctor about the paper containing a poisonous substance.

"I think it's clear that someone is watching you. And even though you'll have me with you from now on, I need you to be more vigilant and cognizant of your surroundings."

"Okay. That's an easy ask. So you being around from now on, what exactly does that look like?"

"With your permission, my team will install security cameras at all accessible entry points at your home in addition to me doing a physical check before you enter every day. And essentially, wherever you go, I go. I'll keep a safe distance, but I won't let you out of my sight."

Ava sighed, and he could see a wave of sadness wash over her features, though she tried to hide her disappointment with a toothless smile.

"It's not forever, and we'll work to get this wrapped up as soon as we can so you can go on your dates."

Ava laughed. The melodious sound warmed his heart.

"So what happens if I want to go on a date before you find who's behind this?"

"Ever heard the phrase *three's a crowd*?"

Ava's mouth flew open. And if he had to describe what he saw in her eyes, he'd liken it to her seeing a ghost walk into the room. Zack chuckled.

"You can date, but I'd have to run a full background check on him, and I'll need an itinerary of events. Even still, someone from my team—even if it isn't me—will be nearby. We can't take any more chances."

"You sound like my father."

"Maybe so, but keep in mind that every choice I make regarding you is for your safety. Someone was close enough to you tonight to poison you, and I don't like that, especially considering I was at the restaurant, too."

That fact was what troubled Zack most. How had something like this gotten past him? He whipped out his phone to text his brother Zeke requesting that he go to the restaurant and secure camera footage. Zack didn't want to leave Ava's side just yet.

"You seem like a man of your word, and my father trusts you and your firm, so I trust your choices are for my good."

A male nurse strolled into the room carrying a replacement bag of fluid for Ava. Zack's initial instinct was that something was off about the man. Nothing about him would make Zack believe the man was a nurse. Though he hated to be stereotypical, this bulky man looked like he'd be more comfortable in a motorcycle club than in a pair of ill-fitting scrubs. The man had only been in the room a minute, and he'd adjusted the scrubs five times. Zack crooked his head to the side to get a look at the man's ID badge, which wasn't visible.

"What's your name?"

"Maverick."

"How long have you been a nurse?" Zack asked.

"About five years," the man mumbled. His face mask prevented Zack from hearing him clearly and from seeing his face. He went through the motions of switching out the bags, though the one in place wasn't near empty.

Zack looked at Ava. Had this been the same nurse who attended to her earlier? Sure, nurses rotated schedules, but he couldn't shake the fact that something was off about the man.

"What's that you're giving her?"

"Just following the doctor's orders, sir," the man answered, but continued his work.

"Stop. We want to see the doctor, so we'll know exactly what he's ordered you to give her."

Ava shot him a worried glance.

If his instincts were off base on this one, then he could deal with that, but what he couldn't handle was someone attempting to hurt Ava in his face.

The male nurse hesitated, looking from Zack to Ava, but relented and stepped away. He stormed out of the room, his heavy steps echoing on the tile floor. When he cleared the room, Zack said, "Something isn't right. I didn't spot a badge, and your current fluid level is three quarters full. Why would he be changing it?"

Ava glanced up at the bags hanging on the poll. The nurse had left them both.

"You don't think…"

Ava didn't finish her sentence. The thought of someone being bold enough to walk into her room to finish the job was a lot to take in. Even for him. But he'd seen worse things happen. More than ten minutes passed before another nurse entered to check on Ava.

"Where's the doctor?" Zack demanded, though he could look at the woman and see she was an employee at the hospital. Her name and picture were visible on her badge, which was clipped near her chest. Amanda Mullins.

A confused expression laced her features. "I wasn't aware you wanted to see the doctor."

"One of your male nurses, Maverick, just came by to change Ava's fluid bag." Zack pointed to the extra bag now hanging on the pole.

The nurse brushed past Zack to Ava's side and examined the bag. "There is no male nurse by the name of Maverick on our staff."

Zack described the man, and she shook her head.

He didn't care that she had other patients to look after. To him, the only one who mattered right now was Ava.

"Stay with her until I get back."

∞

Ava's belly dived to her feet as she watched Zack race out of the room to find the perpetrator. How much nerve and desire for vengeance did someone need to disguise themselves as a nurse, come into her hospital room, and attempt to do what, poison her again? And why her of all people?

Ava swallowed the ache in her throat. She almost didn't want to know the answer, but she needed confirmation. Just how serious was this situation? "What's in that bag?"

The nurse removed it from the pole. "There's no way for me to know just by looking at it. It's no different from the one you have. See." She held both bags in Ava's line of vision.

Sure enough, Ava couldn't tell the difference. She didn't even know which one was real. "But for your safety, we'll replace the fluids." The nurse asked Ava to describe the person and relayed that information to security and her supervisor using the phone in Ava's room. Afterward, she paged the nurse's station and requested another intravenous bag with Ava's prescribed medications. She also gave strict instructions to the nurse on the other line to complete the task.

The nurse removed the tubing and set the IV pole aside.

"Are you comfortable? Can I get you more pillows or adjust your bed?"

Poor woman was just as surprised as Ava and looked like she didn't know what to do with herself. She was probably thinking about her other patients and the laundry list of other duties she had to get to.

"Do they train you all for situations like this?"

"I'd be lying if I said they did. Security is usually tight. However, my boss requested we test the contents of the bag, although I don't know how comforting that is for you. The thought of someone getting past the guards and impersonating a nurse is scary, but it looks like your significant other won't allow anything to happen to you."

"Oh no, he's not…he's just a friend, that's all." Ava didn't want to explain the entire situation. She was still trying to wrap her mind around everything she'd learned and what had happened over the past few hours.

"A very handsome and protective friend. We could all use one like him," she said and wriggled her eyebrows.

Ava didn't know much about Zack, but could readily admit that she was thankful to have him around. She probably wouldn't have thought twice about a nurse coming in to change her IV fluids. And that could've been the end of her.

"Forgive me if I'm overstepping…" Nurse Mullins started.

Here it comes.

Ava knew the questions were coming. She was surprised she didn't ask when Zack left the room.

"Why would someone be trying to kill you? Some of the other nurses and I looked you up when your tox screening came back and saw that you had rat poisoning in your system. You work for your family's handbag company, right? So that doesn't give off any gotta-off-you kind of vibes." She lowered her voice to a whisper.

"Did you kill someone? Sleep with someone's husband? Sell drugs?"

The woman clearly spent her off days streaming drama movies. But Ava couldn't blame her. She'd likely assume the same thing if she were the nurse.

Ava snickered. "No. None of that. Though this situation would probably make more sense if any of those were true. So hopefully my handsome, protective friend can help me figure this out."

"Kinda wish I was in a little bit of trouble if I'd have someone looking like him to help me."

Ava and the nurse shared a laugh, but Ava found herself slightly offended. Why? She couldn't put a finger on it. She'd known the man five minutes, and she had no claim to him.

The door creaked open, and another nurse walked in with her ID badge clearly in view, something that Ava would forever look for now. Nurse Samantha Stevens. The stout blonde handed the IV bag to Nurse Mullins, offered Ava a sympathetic smile, and left the room.

Great. I'll be the topic of conversation for the next few days.

Nurse Mullins went through the motions of connecting the new IV bag to Ava's tubing and hanging it on the pole.

"Following this incident, I'm sure we'll have some kind of training."

That's comforting, though the odds of something like this happening to another patient anytime soon were remote. By the time it did happen, they'd need training again.

Ava nodded and half-listened to Nurse Mullins continue about trainings and protocol—or she could have been talking about something else. Ava's thoughts shifted to Zack. He'd been away at least thirty minutes, though it felt more like two hours. Had he found the perpetrator? If so, was this over? Would it have been the same person behind the rat poisoning in the restaurant? Or the tissue in her car door?

The door creaked open again. This time Zack strolled through. The man could easily pass for a cover model, bodyguard edition. His eyes were squinted and held this serious look, a look that made her worried. Yet, there was a certain warmth there that assured her she was safe with him.

He huffed. "There was no sign of him. It's like he was a ghost. No one saw him. There were no images of him on cameras from what I've seen so far. That's impossible. I don't understand how something like this could happen unless he was working with someone, and I honestly don't believe this person is that smart."

Zack nodded toward the nurse. "Thank you for staying with Ava. I've got it from here. And can we get that bag tested? I want to know what's in it."

"Yes, sir. I called my boss when you left, and he's already given the orders. I'll get the results to you ASAP."

She collected the IV bags, turned, and winked at Ava before leaving the room.

Talk about a romantic. How could the woman even think about romance when Ava's life was in danger?

Zack reclaimed the seat next to her bedside. "How are you?"

"I'm okay. Nurse Mullins switched out my fluids, so I think I'll be okay."

"Good."

"And thank you, Zack. If you weren't here, I probably would be on my way to the morgue if whatever was in that fluid was meant to hurt me. I didn't think twice about him coming in here. He looked official to me."

"You're welcome. It's just instinct. Something seemed off about him the moment he walked in here. I have nothing against male nurses, but he just didn't seem like the type. Plus, I didn't see an ID badge."

"Yeah, after you pointed that out, I noticed the nurses wearing them near their chest in a way that's visible."

"Right. And it's my job to be aware of the little things. Remember, I'm here to protect you."

Zack's phone vibrated, and he excused himself while he accepted the call.

"Got anything?" Zack asked.

Ava could vaguely hear the voice on the other end of the line. She could only be certain that it was a man. And judging by Zack's creased eyebrows, he didn't like the news the man reported. He kept his eyes on Ava while the man spoke.

"Impossible." Zack rubbed his free palm over his face. "Okay…Appreciate it…We'll talk in the morning."

"What's the matter?"

The way his eyes focused on her during the call made her believe the conversation was about her.

"My brother Zeke is at the restaurant. There isn't any camera footage during the time you were there. In fact, the cameras were out of service."

Ava's heart slammed in her chest. The numbers on the heart rate monitor increased. The more information she received, the scarier the situation became. Whoever this person was had a plan and had no qualms about executing it if they didn't get what they wanted. Just what exactly could her father do about these accusations, and how fast could he do it?

Zack covered her hands with his. "I know this might seem scary, but we'll find out who's behind this. As hard as it might seem, try to relax. We have a security guard posted up outside your door. No one can enter without a valid ID and reason. I'll be here all night to double check once the security guard deems it okay for them to enter. No one will hurt you as long as I'm around. That's a promise."

Once again, Zack's touch spread heat through her limbs, calmed her, and made her nervous all at once. She wanted him to keep his hand there, but that was inappropriate. He was her bodyguard. She was his client. Nothing could come of this. Besides, this attraction could be one-sided. Or worse. She could be experiencing these weird emotions because he saved her tonight.

Twice.

But one look in his eyes assured her that wasn't the reason. There was a story behind his intense eyes, and she wanted to hear it.

Chapter Four

"I take it last night was the most hump-day excitement you've had in a while. And I can't say I'm mad at seeing the luggage under your eyes," Zeke announced as he entered Zack's office. He was dressed in his usual polo shirt and khaki slacks with his arms folded across his chest. A satisfied grin spread across his face.

Zack yawned. His brother Zeke's assessment wasn't wrong. Zack had been comfortable behind the desk for more than four years assigning cases and maintaining their firm's books. He kept a watchful eye on Ava last night, only closing his eyes a few minutes at a time, not wanting to risk another nurse perpetrator coming in to finish Ava off.

The doctor released her early that morning when he determined the poison was cleared from her system and there weren't any lasting side effects. Ava only went home to change clothes. According to her, staying home wasn't much of an option. She needed to work to maintain her sanity, so Zack agreed. He trailed her home; performed a sweep of her house for bugs, cameras, or anything out of place. Satisfied, he gave her the all-clear to enter and get cleaned up. He trailed her to work and repeated his actions in her assigned office.

Before he left, Zack gave strict instructions for her not to engage anyone outside of her family, nor eat or drink anything given to her by her assistant or anyone else. Her eyelids fluttered at his request. She'd looked as if she was about to retort, but he figured memories of the previous evening flooded her thoughts, so she relented and offered a half-hearted smile.

Of all the cases he worked prior to chaining himself to the desk, this one had him more baffled. Even if the sweatshop accusations were true, why threaten to kill or attempt bodily harm? It just didn't make sense. However, one thing he'd learned over the years was that criminals were everywhere, and the Langston Brands' handbag business was apparently no exception.

Zack blew a slow stream of air. "Oh yeah. I may have forgotten just how much excitement there is out there."

Zeke sat on the edge of Zack's desk, leaned forward and tagged Zack's shoulder. "Which is why I had to force your hand. You need to be out in the field. That's why we started this business. And before you say anything, Janine can handle the administrative stuff. That's why we hired her. She's basically getting paid to do nothing since you've taken over."

"I'd argue that she's useful. Look at her." Zack nodded toward the glass panels in his office. He had a prime view of the receptionist area and their office entrance.

43

Zeke turned to look at Janine. "She's clicking around on the computer, likely checking her social media."

Zack chuckled. "Then why haven't you fired her?"

Zeke shifted on the desk, returning his attention to Zack. "Probably because she's our cousin. Secondly, I kept holding on to hope that you'd get back out in the field. Given you stayed with the Langston woman all night, I'd like to think we're headed in the right direction."

"Which reminds me. You were the one who set up the contract with Lamont Langston. Why didn't you personally see to Ava's safety?"

Zeke hiked an eyebrow. "Ava?"

Zack waved his hand, brushing off the perplexed look on Zeke's face. "She asked that I refer to her as Ava and not Miss Langston."

"You've already broken your number one rule. Wasn't it you who said you never call your clients by their first name because it starts to blur the lines of the professional relationship?"

"Where is this going? How I refer to her isn't important. I'm just curious as to why you accepted the job and passed it on to me. What about the twins?"

Zeke huffed and shot Zack one of those looks that said he knew the answer to his own question. "We're all tied up on other assignments. Besides, this seemed light enough to help you ease back into the game."

Zack shook his head.

"Seriously, man." Zeke's tone softened. "It's been more than four years since Mariah was killed. You gotta stop blaming yourself and move on. You've put your life on hold for too long. We've given you time to grieve, but you still have a life to live."

"You don't think I know that?"

Zack's voice raised several octaves higher than he intended. But the mere thought of Mariah's senseless death brought back painful memories. He'd left his own wife vulnerable while he was out protecting someone else.

Zeke threw his palms up. "Hey, not trying to offend you, but it's the truth you need to hear."

Zack nodded. He knew more than anyone that he needed to move on, but he'd been paralyzed since Mariah's death.

"I'll tell you what. See Miss Langston—excuse me, Ava's— case through to the end. If you still feel like you aren't ready, I won't bother you again. You and Janine can hold it down here if that's what you want to do. But I've got a feeling this will be good for you. Deal?"

Zack agreed with their brotherly secret handshake, one they'd been doing since elementary school. One clap on both sides of their hands before a firm grip, followed by two shakes. "Deal."

Zeke stood from the spot he'd occupied on the corner of Zack's desk as if his job was done. He strolled toward the door, but turned to face Zack before leaving and leaned against the doorjamb. "So what's your initial assessment of Miss—" he corrected himself— "Ava's situation?"

Zack leaned back in his seat and rubbed the stubble under his chin. On a normal morning, he would've shaved before coming into the office.

"It seems unreal. I haven't been out of the game for that long. Think about the facts. We have a family who owns a luxury handbag business, and suddenly the father receives threatening letters because of some sweatshop accusation. Then there are three incidents of attempted poisonings in one night. Two before she left the restaurant and the other in the hospital. The fluid in the hospital bag the fake nurse tried to give her was ethylene glycol. And what's even more insane, no cameras picked up anything. And no one saw anything."

"You spent fifteen years on the police force. Think about all the times you reported to a crime scene, and there were no eyewitnesses. Doesn't seem that farfetched."

"There's something Lamont didn't tell us. This all seems a bit much for owners of a handbag business, don't you think?"

"It could be that it isn't so much as about the business, but the people involved. Dig below the surface, Zack. Get to know Ava and her family. There are three sisters, so why not the other two? Why not go after Lamont himself or his wife?"

"I've asked myself the same questions."

"Review the file again. Crystal was just in the news for the accused murder of her ex-husband not long ago. There could be something there."

"The answer is in the details," they said simultaneously.

Zeke tapped on the door before he left.

Get to know Ava and her family. That wasn't difficult. Zack had spent time in undercover operations to gather information on many occasions. Before Mariah's death, he'd been doing just that—spending an extensive amount of time with his client to figure out why his family was being killed off one by one. And his client was next. One of his client's brothers was a political official who made side deals with the wrong people. As a result of the brother's deal and not keeping his promise, his family paid the price, except for Zack's client. But in Zack's mind, saving one man's life cost him the love of his life—Mariah.

If only I'd been there for her.

His duty to protect Ava wouldn't be a difficult job, but he couldn't ignore the fact that something transpired between them when their hands touched—stirred something within him that he hadn't allowed himself to feel since Mariah's death. But he had to keep his head clear. Ava wasn't Mariah, and he wasn't doing this job to redeem himself for failing her.

He had to do this job to move on—a steppingstone to free himself from his past.

∞

For the past hour, Ava engaged in a stare down with her computer screen. Work eluded her this morning. Hours ago, she convinced Zack that being in the office would help keep her mind off the attempts on her life, but all she could think about were the poisoning and attempted poisoning.

47

She hadn't eaten anything since she'd left the hospital, and now she was starved. But the mere thought of grabbing anything from anywhere curbed her hunger. How could she trust that there wouldn't be another attempt on her life? Would it happen today if she placed an order to go from the nearest restaurant? Was someone watching her?

Ava rested her head in her palms. She had to find a way not to allow yesterday's events to consume her.

"Hey, hey, hey," Rick Fuller, Langston Brands' vice president announced himself. He knocked and poked his head through the half-opened door without an invitation. Typical Rick.

Maybe I need to be more specific. I need a distraction, but not Rick. He rubbed her the wrong way all the time, acting as if he, instead of her family, owned the company. And what a mistake it was to allow him to temporarily serve as CEO while Crystal had to separate herself from the company. He'd gotten a taste of being at the top, and he'd been an even worse executive ever since. She and her sisters wished her dad would replace him, but he thought Rick added value to the company. He was alone in that thought process.

"Hi, Rick. What can I do for you?" Ava said through a forced smile.

"How did things go last night? My assistant notified me that our morning meeting was cancelled."

Dressed in a tailored black suit with a white button-down shirt, black slacks, and a red tie, Rick stepped all the way into her office and stood in front of her desk.

Ava refrained from rolling her eyes and squinted at Rick for several seconds. Did he not know that she'd been poisoned? But then it dawned on her that her family likely didn't want to broadcast that information. Besides, anyone could be a suspect. Especially those who had knowledge of her whereabouts. Suspicion rose within her about Rick, but she squashed the thought before it completely formed. The man was high strung on becoming CEO, and he wouldn't do anything that could potentially harm his chances.

"It was interesting. Ms. Wertheimer mentioned sweatshop accusations about our overseas manufacturing operations. Know anything about that?"

Rick slouched in the visitor's seat across from her desk, crossed an ankle over his knee, and dismissed her comment with a wave of his hand. "That's nothing new. Many U.S. companies are accused of the same thing every year. What does that have to do with anything?"

"This is serious, Rick."

Ava leaned forward and glared at him. His behavior was contradictory to what she thought it would be, especially for someone who wouldn't hesitate to run her family's company.

"Yeah, but it's nothing we can't deal with. I spoke to your father about an hour ago. He's on a flight this evening to check on the operations in Cambodia himself. That should help clear things up."

Ava tilted her head and eyed him. "How long have you known about these accusations, and why didn't you say anything to me before I went into that meeting last night?"

"I honestly had no idea it would even come up, but Elaine taught you well, so I'm sure you handled it like a champ. My focus is getting Langston Brands' sales back on track since our latest collection flopped. Who cares about some sweatshop rumors anyway?"

"I do, and you should have mentioned it to me so that I could've been prepared. How long have you known?"

"Not long. A couple of months."

Ava slapped her hand against the desk. "Months? When were you planning to tell any of us?"

"I talked to your father. You should be asking him why he didn't say anything to you." One side of Rick's mouth turned up. Ava wanted to reach across the desk and pull his lips off. Was it his goal to embarrass her?

Calm down.

"In the future," Ava said, speaking through clenched teeth, "please inform me if there are any situations that might affect any distribution deals I'm working on. Are we clear?"

"You've got it. So," Rick leaned forward with his elbows on his knees and clapped, "what did Wertheimer say? Is the sweatshop fiasco going to stop them from including the bags in their new stores?"

Had she been sitting in the office talking to the wall the last few minutes? This man was unbelievable.

"How about I just keep you posted?"

Rick stood and winked. "Please do."

"I'll be in touch." Ava turned her attention to the laptop screen, which had gone into standby mode, hoping Rick would get the picture and leave her be. She didn't know what to make of him today. When he entered her office, he seemed concerned about the meeting, then when she mentioned the sweatshop accusations, he didn't seem bothered. However, right before he left, his voice turned serious. She couldn't be affected by Rick's antics today though. She'd just let Crystal deal with him since she was the CEO and worked more with Rick anyway.

Rick walked out of her office, but before shutting the door, it opened again. Air filled Ava's chest, and she'd prepared to tell him to leave her alone, but it was Zack who appeared in her doorway. His leather jacket and bald head grabbed her attention, and she found herself wondering if his head was as smooth as it looked.

Her agitation with Rick dissipated when she locked eyes with Zack.

What is it about this man that makes my heart speed?

"I wasn't expecting to see you back here so soon," Ava said.

Zack held up the plastic bag he carried. "I brought you lunch. I hear your favorite is sushi."

"Only if it's shrimp tempura or a salmon roll."

Zack nodded and smile. "Then I'm right on the money."

He strolled to her desk, removed her food from the bag, and handed her the containers. "Mind if I stick around and eat with you?"

"How could I even think about saying no when you're feeding me?"

Zack chuckled—a chuckle that made her freeze her rummaging through the takeout container. She glanced up at him and smiled, but reminded herself to dial it down. He was only there because he was being paid to do so. Nothing more.

"Smart woman, but still, if you were in the middle of something, I can come back at our agreed time to make sure you get home alright."

"You're good. Please have a seat."

The aroma of chicken fried rice and the shrimp tempura rolls satisfied her senses, making her forget that moments ago she was afraid to eat anything.

She watched Zack bow his head before taking his first bite. When he looked up, she said, "Thank you for thinking of me."

"You're welcome. I figured it might cheer you up and give me an opportunity to learn more about you and your family. We'll be working closely together, which means you'll be seeing a lot of me. It'll help me work your case if I know more about the Langstons. A lot of times, the answer is closer than we think."

Ava prayed over her own food before stuffing a shrimp tempura roll in her mouth, savoring the crunchy shrimp, avocado, and rice. It was so good that she probably would've danced in her seat if she were alone.

"Okay. I'll tell you whatever you want to know if it means this nightmare will be over soon."

"Talk to me about you and your duties here. How long have you worked for your family's company, and why did you chose this path?"

"I've been here since I finished college eighteen years ago after I earned a business degree in marketing from Jackson State University. I've only been the sales director for the past five years. Before my dad would make me sales director, I had to do a rotation in finance, marketing, management, manufacturing, and sales. We all had to. My father thought it was important that we received a well-rounded view of the business."

She could've sworn she saw a small smile appear on the corners of his lips, but it disappeared just as quickly as it appeared. His expression became serious again.

"Tell me what happened to Crystal a few months ago—the situation with her and her ex-husband."

Ava recounted the situation as she knew it, with Crystal attending her twentieth college class reunion. The night ended with her charged with Dante's murder. The charges were dropped, but her nightmare didn't end there. The woman Dante was seeing, along with the woman's cousin who was also Dante's agent attempted to frame Crystal for Dante's murder, stalked Crystal, kidnapped her, and ultimately threatened to murder her.

Zack ate his own food and listened to Ava recount the details. His intense eyes tripped her up a few times. She hoped he didn't think she made any of that up.

"And did anything come up about your family's company in the middle of that drama?"

"No, not that I can think of. I was overseas at the time working on a distribution deal with a retailer in Paris. The only issue that I'm aware of was that since Crystal is CEO, it brought about negative publicity."

"And now someone is attempting to bring more negative publicity to your family's company with these new sweatshop rumors." Zack finished her thought.

"Right."

He nodded. "Okay. Now tell me about Layla."

"She doesn't get into much of anything, though she's vocal about everything—saying what she feels when she feels like it—but she doesn't get into any trouble. There isn't anything in her background that would cause any of this."

Zack dug deeper by asking questions about each sister's relationships. Crystal was the only one dating, but she'd known Marcel Singleton most of her life. He couldn't have anything to do with the accusations against Langston Brands or Ava's poisoning. He was more like a brother to her.

"Ever met any of the shareholders? Based on the letters your father received, we're thinking whoever is behind this is one of the shareholders with a large investment in your company."

Zack's question caught Ava with a mouthful of sushi. She shook her head. Once she swallowed, she said, "I wouldn't have any idea who any of the shareholders were if they walked into this room."

"That's expected. We're going to get that information though and start digging into their backgrounds."

Zack questioned her about her daily routine and that of her family, including her father. She didn't think that would provide much help, but Zack encouraged her to share whatever she knew. They'd never know when something would be important.

Though unexpected, Zack's presence made her more comfortable. His eyes held a hint of understanding and softness, and though he knew more about her than she knew about him, she had no doubt that she could trust him.

The only trouble with her trusting him was that she hoped it didn't lead to her falling for a man who was getting paid to spend time with her.

Chapter Five

Learning that Ava wasn't involved in a serious relationship surprised yet relieved Zack. He'd be lying to himself if he said knowing that information was solely for their working relationship. Though it was true that he wouldn't have to worry about a jealous, insecure man's concerns about him and Ava spending so much time together and impeding his investigation, her unattachment could mean that she'd be open to dating him when this situation was behind them.

If he was even ready for a such a thing.

Mariah still monopolized his thoughts most days.

Zack packed their empty containers back into the bag. "Everything you shared was helpful. I'll put these away and get out of your hair for a while so you can get some work done. I'll be back thirty minutes before you're ready to leave. Four-thirty, right?"

Ava wiped her mouth with a napkin. "Right. And thanks again for lunch."

"You're welcome. See you in a little while."

Zack strolled toward the door. When he reached for the knob, it twisted, and the door opened. Zack took a few steps back, and Lamont walked through.

"Great. You're still here. Just the person I need to talk to. Well, I need to talk to both of you."

Lamont darted his eyes between the two of them. Discomfort settled there, much like the way he looked in the hospital emergency room while they waited to hear news about Ava. He advanced across the office and claimed one of the visitor's chairs across from Ava's desk and waved Zack back to the area he'd just vacated. "Come, sit. I have more news to share with you."

Zack took the visitor's chair next to Lamont, still warm from when he occupied it moments ago. He glanced at Ava who now sat erect in her seat with wide eyes. Seconds ago, she'd been more relaxed with a smile plastered across her face. Now she was poised for bad news. Zack couldn't lie, so was he. Why else would Lamont want to talk to them?

"I'll be leaving the office shortly and heading straight to the airport for this dreaded international flight."

"I probably should be going with you," Ava said.

"No." Lamont's tone was abrupt, but he said what Zack was about to say: Was she out of her mind?

"Dad, it isn't the worse idea, especially when this matter is affecting the work I do here. This company means just as much to me as it does to you. And if something is wrong overseas, I want to help fix it."

"And the only thing I want for you is to stay safe. You're in good hands with Zack and The Four Kings. I have no doubts about that. If the manufacturing conditions aren't up to par over there, I'll make sure we get it right. Crystal and I have already agreed that I'll handle it."

Zack sensed there was something more to Lamont's story— something he wasn't sharing.

"What else is going on?" Zack asked.

Lamont looked at Ava, then removed an envelope from inside his suit jacket and handed it to Zack.

"What's that?"

Zack skimmed the note, then read it aloud.

Don't test me. Langston Brands' stock prices are falling every day. FIX IT. I don't have to tell you what'll happen if you don't. Ava might not be so lucky next time.

Zack's blood traipsed through his veins causing his skin to grow warmer by the second. This person was a bully, and he despised bullies.

Lamont focused his attention on Ava. "That's one of the reasons why you shouldn't go with me. I don't know what's with this person, but I feel better knowing we have Zack to protect you."

Ava folded her arms across her chest and rested her elbows on the mahogany oversized executive desk. "Who's going to protect you? Will you have security detail while you're away?"

"Yes, I will, but you're my primary concern since the letters seem to be focused on you."

Something Zack needed to figure out. What was it about Ava that made her the target and not any of the other members of her family?

Ava locked eyes with Zack, and he tried to understand what she didn't say. She'd shared details about her past with him, but Zack had to wonder what the complete story was behind her captivating eyes. He swallowed down his momentary lack of focus and licked his lips.

"And we'll get to the bottom of it. That's my promise to both of you. I won't allow anything to happen to you, Ava."

Zack folded the letter and stuffed it in his own jacket pocket. He'd check it for fingerprints and run them through their database back at his office.

Lamont shook Zack's hand. "I have complete faith in your abilities. I worked with your father for years in the army and even after my honorable discharge. I'm certain he's ingrained some of his skills into his sons, so I'm confident you're well equipped to handle this. You're from good stock, trained well."

"Thank you, sir."

Lamont stood and rounded the desk to where Ava sat, rigid. He bent over and wrapped his arm around his shoulders. "Everything will be alright, sweetheart. You'll see. I love you, and I'll give you all a call when our flight arrives."

Ava kissed his cheek. "Love you, too. Please be safe."

"Always."

59

Lamont tapped Zack's shoulder on his way out of Ava's office. When Lamont closed the door behind him and they were alone again, Zack studied Ava. Her eyes were glazed over with a far-off look, and she'd returned to guarding herself with her arms threaded across her chest. She'd been stuck in that position for the past few minutes. Zack hadn't been one to need protection in his life, but he'd provided services to enough clients to imagine what Ava might be experiencing right now. Fear. Uncertainty. Disbelief.

"Need me to stay here with you for a while?"

Ava snapped her head in his direction. The focus returned to her eyes. "No. I'll be fine here. We can stick with our plan for you to come back later. I'm okay," she reassured him.

"Have time to give me a tour of the office?"

Ava crooked her head to the side, and Zack explained further. "It'll give me an opportunity to look around for anything suspicious without looking suspicious if I have you as an escort."

She smiled. "Makes sense. I need to stretch my legs anyway. I've been sitting all morning." Ava closed her laptop lid, stood, and rounded the desk. "Come. I'd be happy to give you an office tour."

Zack grabbed the plastic bag filled with their empty food containers and followed Ava out of her office. This tour would give him a chance to see how other employees responded to Ava. One could never be too sure about who to trust in situations like this. The person behind these threats could be working with someone in the office, and if that were the case, he'd sniff out any suspicious characters in minutes.

∞

Nervous energy crawled through Ava's veins. Hopefully Zack wasn't beginning to think she was some kind of weirdo. Her legs wobbled with each step through the office corridor. Could she even produce a smile fake enough for Langston Brands employees to believe? Someone would catch on to the fact that something was off about her. It wasn't like she walked visitors through the office often, especially one of the opposite sex. She tossed her raging thoughts aside. Maybe they'd think she'd decided to get involved with someone. Ava released the thoughts with a sly shrug and squared her shoulders, exuding a level of confidence she was lacking.

"This floor is primarily our accounting and finance staff. Crystal and Rick, our VP's offices are on this floor as well."

Ava led him past the first group of accounting staff members and Rick's office. She'd had enough of him today so she wasn't planning to stop there.

Zack spoke in a tone low enough for only her ears. "And this Rick. You trust him?"

As far as I can throw him.

Ava matched his tone. "My dad does. He's been loyal to the company since he started seven years ago."

Zack nodded and gave Rick a quick once-over as they passed his open door. Ava looked straight ahead.

Next to Rick's office was the Clutch conference room. Each of their conference rooms was named after the company's different styles of handbags—Satchel, Tote, Wristlet, Clutch, and Crossbody—and like the size of the bag, the Tote conference room was the largest and big enough to comfortably sit their two hundred employees. The Satchel held about one hundred. The Crossbody and Hobo could both seat twenty-five people. The Wristlet and Clutch were the two smallest rooms, which could seat about ten people.

Ava stepped inside the Clutch conference room and flicked on the light to give Zack a quick preview. A silver tray with ten white ceramic coffee mugs sat in the middle of the table next to a vase of fresh flowers. Apple cinnamon filled the air. Every time she went inside the Clutch, thoughts of orange and red leaves coupled with her snuggled in her favorite chair sipping hot chocolate danced in her mind.

"Nice. Smells good, too."

Ava led him past another group of employees nestled in cubicles, clicking away at their keyboards and to Crystal's office.

"Patrice, is Crystal free for a few minutes?"

Patrice Wilkins, Crystal's assistant, clicked around her screen to open Crystal's calendar. "Yes. Looks like it. Her next meeting isn't for another thirty minutes."

"Thanks."

"You're welcome," Patrice said, but her eyes were glued to Zack.

"Oh, I'm being a little rude today. This is Zack Kingsland. He'll be helping me out with a few things for a while."

Ava didn't think she'd ever seen Patrice smile so wide. "Nice to meet you, Mr. Kingsland. I'm Patrice Wilkins."

Zack shook her hand. "Nice meeting you, Ms. Wilkins."

"Please call me Patrice."

"Noted."

Ava tapped on Crystal's door and waited for her response before entering. "Hey. I have a special guest with me today."

Zack walked in behind Ava and shut the door.

Crystal's eyebrows shot up, but she quickly recovered. She obviously wasn't expecting to see Zack in the office, which was one of the reasons Ava thought it would be a good idea for her and Zack to stop by to say hello. "Good to see you again, Zack. Thank you for taking care of my sister."

"You're welcome. It's what I do."

There it went again. Why did it bother her that the only reason he was there was because he was obligated to do so?

"So, what are you two up to? Anything new? Did Dad stop by to see you on his way out?"

Zack and Ava sat in the visitors' chairs across from Crystal's desk. "Yes. We saw Dad and the new letter he received. I'm giving Zack a little tour of our offices. It might help him to get a look around to see if anything or anyone seems suspect."

"Sounds like a good idea to me, but wait…about this letter. What did it say?" Crystal's forehead and eyebrows wrinkled.

Zack didn't hesitate to answer Crystal. "Much of the same, but I'm going to take it back to the office to see if we can get prints."

Crystal's eyes glossed over. "I hate you're going through this. Trust me. I know how crazy this can be, but with someone like Zack who is trained for this sort of thing, I believe you'll be fine."

Ava recognized a hint of fear in Crystal's voice and that she spoke to convince herself as well as Ava.

Zack leaned forward and rested his elbows on his knees. "The thing about people like this is that they always mess up somewhere along the way. Never fails. They've already given us some sort of hint on how to find them because of their interest in Langston Brands' stock. Whoever this person is must have a lot to lose. We'll start by pulling a record of your stockholders and investigating those with the largest investment."

"With that plan, this'll all be over soon," Crystal said.

Crystal's phone rang. She peeked over to check the caller's name. "I need to take this, unless you have something else you want to discuss."

"No. I'm all good. Zack?"

"I don't have anything else. Do what you need to do." He stood. "Good seeing you again, Miss Langston."

She lifted the phone and covered the mouthpiece of the receiver. "It's Crystal."

Zack gave her a thumbs-up and trailed Ava out of Crystal's office. They said their good-byes to Patrice, Crystal's assistant, and continued around the hall.

After leading him around the rest of the floor, Ava said, "We're all done here. Marketing and publicity is one floor down and also where Layla sits. We'll go there next."

"You're the boss. I'm following you."

A flirtatious fleeting thought crossed through Ava's mind, but she didn't verbalize it. Instead, she smiled and waved Zack toward the elevator bank. Confident they were the only two in the area, Ava asked, "Notice anything?"

"No. Typically, if someone in the area knew anything, seeing someone out of the ordinary like me might make them nervous, jittery, or cause them to look over their shoulder. None of them gave me a second thought."

"Except for maybe Patrice," Ava added in a sing-song voice.

Zack erupted in a lighthearted chuckle, and it made Ava's heart smile to see the not-so-serious side of him. "Nah."

"I take it you're used to that sort of thing—women ogling you."

"Nah. Don't get that a lot."

The elevator arrived, and they stepped on. Ava pressed the button for the sixth floor. "Modest. I like that."

When they arrived on the sixth floor, they went through similar motions, with Ava walking Zack around the floor passing employees in the cubicles. Their dad's office door was closed and so was their mom's. She'd accompanied him on the international trip. Their marketing director's office was next to Layla's. Ava stopped in to introduce Zack to Jackie Tucker. She smiled and shook his hand, but didn't fawn over him the way Patrice had.

She pointed out the Wristlet and Hobo conference rooms, which were on the opposite side of the floor, before leading him into Layla's office. Ava mentally braced herself for that interaction because she never knew what Layla would say.

Her door was open, but Ava still tapped a few times before entering. "Hey there. Busy?"

Layla looked up from her laptop screen and darted her eyes between Ava and Zack. She closed the laptop. "Never too busy for you," she answered as her lips spread into a huge smile.

"You remember Zack Kingsland? I'm giving him a little tour of our offices."

"A man all over this new assignment. Leave no stone uncovered. I like it."

Ava shot Layla a please-don't-embarrass-me look.

Layla pretended not to notice and kept her attention on Zack. "Good seeing you again, Mr. Kingsland. Please take a seat."

Zack did as instructed. Ava closed the door and took the seat next to him. He jumped right in. "I know we didn't get a chance to talk much last night, but if you notice anything or anyone off or out of place around here, let me know."

"I haven't been aware of anything unusual, but trust I wouldn't hesitate to say something. Just let me know if there's any way I can help, and I'm all for it."

Zack looked between Ava and Layla before he asked, "Are there any questions I can answer for you while I'm here?"

"None right now, but if you can convince Ava to go home and rest, that would be great. I don't think she needs to be here today after what she went through last night."

"And you know work will help me keep my mind off that incident," Ava interjected.

"That might be true for now, but don't forget who you're talking to."

Ava leaped out of her seat. "Okay. Time to go. Let's not bore Zack with your premonitions and whatnot."

"Let's not. I'll just bore you with them later."

Ava and Zack completed the tour of the remaining two floors. She ended the tour in the elevator bank on the first floor.

"Sorry if walking around the office didn't help much."

"Don't be. I now have a good idea of the office layout and the level of access to you. Like I told you, no detail is too small."

"Alright then. Until four-thirty..." Ava extended her palm for a handshake. Again, those tingles gyrated up her arm like a group of people running to the dance floor and moving to the cha-cha slide. Dang it. She was kind of hoping the sensation was a one-off situation, but whatever the man had going on, it connected with her soul, and she had no idea what could be done about it.

"Until four-thirty."

Chapter Six

One week had passed since Ava's poisoning incident, and that was just the way Zack liked it. No threats. No activity. Peace. But he couldn't relax or let his guard down, neither could Ava. No activity could possibly mean that this person only wanted to send a message with the poisoning incident or that they were planning something else. Neither situation gave him any comfort.

As he'd done for the last week, Zack arrived at Langston Brands' downtown Houston office about fifteen minutes before Ava ended her workday. By this time, building security had grown accustomed to seeing him every day. To the untrained eye, it probably looked like they were two people in the early stages of a new relationship with all the time they were spending together. He took her lunch every day, too. The gesture wasn't necessary, but made him feel better knowing her food hadn't been tampered with because he'd seen to it himself.

He sent her a text.

Z: Downstairs in the lobby. I'll wait for you here.

A: Okay. Give me five minutes.

As quickly as he made the decision to wait for her downstairs, he changed his mind. Something felt off. He couldn't describe it. Nothing appeared amiss in the building's lobby. The same three security guards were in place. Other employees strolled out of the building, minding their own business. And the ten people he counted were all wearing their employee badges. The only thing he could lean on was instinct, and instinct said to go to Ava's office.

Z: Never mind. Think I'll come up to get you.

A: That's fine, too.

Zack said hello to the security guards and stated his purpose for entering the Langston Brands office. He handed over his ID, and once given the okay, he strolled to the elevator bank. One of the elevators opened as soon as he entered the area. He hopped on and pressed the button that would take him to Ava's office floor.

When the doors opened, he stepped off and scanned the area. The same serene atmosphere that greeted him the last time he'd visited her office engulfed him. Again, for the employees who were still working, they were engrossed in a world of their own, eyes glued to computer screens with earbuds plugged into their ears.

Zack strolled to Ava's office and rapped on the door three times before entering. Her assistant had already left for the day.

"Hey," Zack greeted her as he strolled inside.

He made it a point to give everyone he spoke to eye contact, but locking eyes with Ava was becoming much more of a task than it should be. Her warm eyes spoke before her lips parted, and the shimmer in her eyes awakened something inside of him. It'd been years since any woman looked at him the way she did—like she was happy to see him. Though the constant interaction, surveillance, and monitoring were difficult for her to deal with a week ago, she seemed to be taking it in stride these days.

"Hey. How are you?" The light in her eyes dimmed. "Is everything all right? Did you find something?"

Zack threw up his palms and claimed a visitor's seat in front of her desk. "Oh, nothing has happened to cause concern. Just moving off instinct."

Ava relaxed her shoulders, and the light in her eyes returned. "Okay. Good."

"Need any help with anything?"

Ava chuckled. "I appreciate the offer, but what exactly could you help me with around here?"

"I can be resourceful. Give me the task, and I can figure something out."

Ava closed her laptop and stuffed it into her oversized bag. "Well, lucky for you I'm wrapping up for the evening, so you don't have to be resourceful today, but I'll keep that in mind when my admin is slipping up or something."

"You can never say I didn't offer."

Ava snorted. "I can think up something for you to do if babysitting me isn't enough."

"This is far from babysitting. More like keeping a watchful eye on you to keep you safe."

"That's exactly what babysitting is. Plus, feeding the person you're looking after, which you've been doing for the last week. By the way, I'm not complaining about the food. It's nice to have someone take care of that for me."

"But something else is bothering you. What is it?"

Ava shoved a file into her bag, then rested her hands on the zipper. She glanced at him and twisted her lips, as if unsure if she should say what was on her mind. She licked her lips and released a heavy breath.

Zack leaned back in his seat and waited. He watched her carefully for everything she didn't say. Reading between the lines was what he'd been trained to do.

"It's just that I feel like it's hard for me to have a social life with this hanging over my head, and I'm having to drag you all around town with me just to do something as simple as go to the grocery store. I can't date right now, not seriously. This is just a lot."

Zack nodded. "I hear you, and I understand, but tell me what the problem is right now. What are you not saying?"

Ava knitted her eyebrows together. "Is it crossing the line if I ask you to be my date to a comedy show tonight?"

Before he could respond, she added, "Not like a *date* date. This is more of me inviting you to come along since you're coming anyway, but to relax a little and enjoy the show kind of thing."

He should say no.

Say no.

But like Ava said, it wasn't a real date, and he'd be tagging along anyway. And he could still enjoy the show and keep an eye on her, too.

Would he be blurring the lines though?

Not a real date. But I should still say no.

He'd obviously taken too long to respond because she said, "I just made this awkward, didn't I?"

Zack stood to reassure her, stopping short of taking her hands into his. Maybe the lines were already slightly blurred. "No, you didn't, and I get it. I'd love to come. It's been years since I've gone to a live comedy show."

"Same here. I just thought I could use a few laughs after everything that's been happening in my life."

"I understand. Just remember that this situation is temporary. Soon enough, it'll be all behind you."

Ava hoisted the designer laptop bag over her shoulder. "And I'm counting on you to make that happen."

When she rounded the desk, Zack slipped the bag off her shoulder. He's carried it every day since this routine started. "Let me get that for you."

"Thanks."

He slipped the bag over his head and shoulder, then led her out of the office and retraced his steps back to the elevator bank.

When they arrived at her car inside the parking garage, he went about his inspection. Tires. Gas tank. Swept the inside for bugs. Checked under the hood for anything out of place. Satisfied, he placed her bag in the passenger seat and opened the driver's side door for her to climb inside.

"Everything looks good."

"Okay. Thanks." She held her breath each time he checked her car, house, or office. He could see her chest deflate before she climbed behind the steering wheel.

"I'll be right behind you." Zack jogged over to his vehicle. Lamont had given him an assigned parking space a few spaces down from Ava's spot. After he started his engine and backed out of the space, Ava did the same, and they proceeded with their routine of him following her home and checking to ensure nothing was out of order.

When he entered her three-bedroom, one-story home this evening, he expected it to be clean and cozy-looking like a model home. Hardly lived in. It smelled of clothes fresh out of the dryer. The most he'd seen out of place was a coffee mug in the sink with an imprint of her red lipstick around the rim.

And everything looked the same as it had for the past week, which gave him some level of comfort. Whoever this person was hadn't attempted to invade her personal space. Hopefully that comforted her, too.

"All clear. I'll be back to pick you up at…"

"Seven," Ava completed his sentence. "That'll give us enough time to get through this traffic, order food, and settle before the opening act."

Her eyes held a hint of excitement. Or was he just imagining the gleam?

"Seven it is."

Zack spun on his heels and left Ava to get ready. As crazy and unprofessional as it sounded, he was looking forward to the evening out with Ava. He hadn't been this close to another woman since Mariah died. And this wasn't a real date, so there was no pressure to impress her, although she hadn't been out in a while either from what he gathered, so he did want this evening to turn out nice for her.

All he had to do was refrain from extended eye contact because every time they locked eyes for more than a few seconds, something stirred within him. And he couldn't have that. No stirrings. No feelings. Just him doing his job to keep Ava safe.

∞

Ava carefully selected a casual outfit—something cute, but not date-like. She couldn't look like she tried too hard, and she also couldn't look like she didn't care about her appearance. Her ensemble had to be a happy medium, so she went with a pair of skinny jeans and riding boots, coupled with a black elbow-length shirt and light cargo jacket. Tonight would likely be her last time wearing the jacket and boots. Spring was around the corner, and Houston's weather was chilly enough to pull them off this evening.

She gave herself a once-over in the mirror. Satisfied with her look, she grabbed her crossbody purse and hung it across her body.

The ringing doorbell caused goosebumps to pop up along her arms, and a seed of doubt sprung into her mind.

We shouldn't do this.

But it was too late to back down now. She had tickets, and Zack was already at her door. Ava released several calming breaths and shook her hands like she was air drying them as she walked to the door.

"Hey. Right on time," she announced when she opened the door.

Zack must have had the same idea she did when it came to dressing for the evening—not too dressed up and not too laid back either. He sported jeans, a black shirt, and that same black leather snakeskin jacket he'd worn since she met him. On anyone else, the jacket would probably make them stand out in the crowd, but it fit Zack like it was designed just for him. Did he ever take it off?

Zack handed her a gift bag. "This is for you."

Why is he making this a real date?

Ava accepted the bag, fished around the tissue paper and peeked inside. Zack bought her a bag of her favorite chocolates, Ghirardelli caramel squares. She gushed. "Thank you. How'd you know?"

"You always have one on your desk in the office."

"That was very thoughtful of you. I'll run these inside and put them away, then I'll be ready."

Ava whisked away, placed the small gift bag on her kitchen counter, and rejoined him at the door.

"Ready."

Zack waited by her side while she locked the door. His cologne smelled like it was designed for him, too—a woodsy, fresh scent that wasn't overpowering, but in fact smelled like it could be his natural body scent, yet it was mesmerizing enough to make her want to fall into his arms. Goodness, where did this man shop? Zacks-R-Us? But this wasn't a date, and she couldn't make this any weirder than she already had by asking him out in the first place.

Though it was a non-date, Zack was still the perfect gentleman and opened the passenger-side door for her and waited until she was inside and strapped in before he closed the door, rounded the car, and climbed behind the wheel.

The thirty-minute drive to the Improv wasn't as awkward as it could've been considering the circumstance. They engaged in surface-level conversation about comedy shows they'd watched in the past and favorite comedians.

A beat of silence passed between them, and Zack took his eyes off the road for a couple of seconds too long in her opinion and glanced at her. "You know I'm curious about why you asked me to come with you. Don't get me wrong, I appreciate the invite. It just seems like there are other people who would be higher up on your list of people to spend time with. Plus, you and your sisters seem close."

He's probably thinking I like him.

Saying that he was last on her list sounded rude, so instead she responded, "We are close, but you had to come anyway, right? Besides, you seem like you could use a good laugh."

He didn't shift his eyes in her direction, but she saw the lift of his right eyebrow. "Is that your way of saying I'm uptight?"

Ava chuckled. "That might not be the word I'd use, but you have to admit that you hardly ever smile."

"Do you feel safe with me?"

"Of course, I do. Why do you ask?"

"Can you honestly say your answer would be the same if I walked around showing all of my teeth?"

Ava erupted into laughter. "You have a point. I'd probably wonder if you were serious. But it's more than just your face. You just have this look—" She pointed at him and wagged her finger up in down— "of a bodyguard. I remember thinking that the first time I saw you in the restaurant. I don't know if my answer would be the same if you smiled all the time."

"I'm gonna go with not. You'd be asking for someone else to take over."

And he'd be right. Besides, knowing his background, there was something about the look of him that made her trust him completely. Some people had *it,* and Zack was one of those people. Before meeting him, she'd say she wasn't even attracted to the biker-looking, muscly, bodyguard-looking type. But this man worked it well.

Ava smoothed her now sweaty palms along her thighs. "Yeah, let's just say you win that one. I guess I'm okay with the straight face."

"If it makes you feel any better, you'll see my teeth tonight if this comedian is funny enough."

Ava smiled, and Zack returned the gesture with his usual one-sided upturned lip. "A little."

When they arrived at the Improv, settled in their seats, and ordered appetizers, Ava eyed him for a moment, trying to determine if she should ask the question that had been burning the back of her brain. Would he perceive it as being too personal since this wasn't a real date? She considered it a fair question since he knew everything about her life.

Zack sipped his water. "You have that look on your face again. What is it?"

"Never mind. I think I have my answer." It only made sense that he wasn't dating anyone. Otherwise, he wouldn't have accepted her invitation for this non-date. A significant other could understand him attending because he was her private security guard, but not as her non-date.

He licked his lips and pressed his weight onto the table with his arms folded across his chest. "I'd rather answer your question than have you speculate."

He narrowed his eyes just a little in way she found attractive. Why was she attracted to almost everything he did? Maybe she really did need to get out more. Perhaps go on a real date.

"Are you dating? Married?"

A darkness flashed across his eyes that almost made her regret asking. The question certainly caused a level of discomfort for him. He looked away toward the stage, took a swig of his water again, then answered, "No, I'm not."

In the brief time she'd known him, he tended to maintain eye contact when speaking with her, but not when she asked about his relationship status. She channeled her inner Layla and pushed. "Why not? Does your work keep you too busy?"

"Work may be the reason I don't have anyone. I lost my wife five years ago while I was out on a case protecting someone else. I should've been home protecting her." He tilted his head and raised an eyebrow as if to ask, *Any more questions?*

But what could she say to that? Surely, he'd heard the phrase *I'm sorry* too many times over the years. Instinctively, she reached out and covered his hand with hers, forgetting about the jolts of electrical charge that followed whenever their hands touched. This time wasn't any different. Zack nodded his thanks, understanding her conveyance of sympathy for his loss. He flipped his hand over and held hers in his palm—the touch both satisfying and terrifying. The emcee's voice boomed into the microphone jolting her to her senses, and she withdrew her hand, tucking it into her lap.

As the evening progressed, Ava hoped she hadn't dampened his mood by causing him to relive his past. Why exactly did he blame himself for what happened to his wife? They stole glances at each other throughout the evening, but she couldn't tell if he was

79

having a good time. He appeared to be on guard every time she looked at him, his eyes constantly darting around the room. Him sizing up their waiter. Or requesting that she only drink bottled water. He ordered the food and then gave it to her because he didn't want anyone to think the food was for her. His back was as rigid as wood. And his teeth? She never saw them. His chest shook a few times, which was her only indication he thought the jokes were funny. She could only chalk it up to the fact that she asked about his relationship status.

The man clearly had some unresolved pain, and she'd do well not to cross any lines with him. But the way her soul responded to his touch, she wasn't sure that wasn't already a lost cause.

Chapter Seven

After dropping Ava off and ensuring her home was secure, Zack went to The Four Kings' office instead of retreating to his own residence. She was starting to get under his skin, and the sooner he could get this case resolved, the better off they both would be. Besides, he wasn't ready to get back to his place just to get in bed and wind up with jumbled thoughts of Mariah and Ava.

He needed time to think and sort through the information they'd obtained so far, go through the shareholder list, do anything other than think about Ava.

"Thought you were gone for the evening," his brother Zeke said as he walked right into Zack's office and plopped in the chair positioned across from Zack's desk.

Zack didn't look up at Zeke. Instead, he kept his focus on his laptop screen. "Came back after taking Ava to the comedy show. Need to work."

"You went on a date with her?" Zeke's voice rose an octave or three.

"Settle down. It wasn't a date." Zack worked to convince himself and Zeke that he hadn't crossed any boundaries with Ava. "She invited me because I'd be there anyway. No big deal."

"Back up, back up, back up. Rewind the tape and hit play."

Zack withdrew from his laptop and blew a frustrated breath.

Frustrated at himself.

Frustrated at Ava for being attractive.

And frustrated at his brother for digging his proverbial nail into his emotional craziness. He rubbed a palm over his face and leaned back in his chair, giving Zeke the same look and energy, he gave to him.

"What do you want me to say?"

Zeke shifted in his seat, seemingly to make himself more comfortable. "I just want to know what's happening to you, bro. If it were one of the twins, maybe something like this wouldn't take me by surprise, but you're by the book. Strait-laced. Like, you were the one who never got into trouble growing up. And now take a step back. Can't you see what's happening?"

Zack shook his head. He wasn't sure what was happening, at least not when it came to Ava. Well, that wasn't entirely true. He liked her, but he couldn't openly admit that without also admitting that he was crossing a dangerous line, which could impair his ability to protect her. Couldn't it? "You seem to know. Why don't you tell me?"

"Why don't you first talk to me about the comedy show. How was it?"

"Alright. I didn't get into it too much. Had to stay vigilant and keep an eye out for anyone questionable. If someone could get to her at a restaurant, they could probably get to her there, too. I didn't allow myself to enjoy it really. Can't be in another situation where I'm not able to do my job."

Zeke opened his mouth, then shut it. Zack knew what his brother wanted to say for the hundredth time, that what happened to Mariah wasn't his fault. Deep down, he knew that to be true, but in his heart, he couldn't reconcile the fact that he could've done something—anything—to protect her. If he'd made a different choice that night, Mariah would still be alive.

"Whether you want to admit it or not, you're changing. Will you promise me one thing?"

Zack hated promises. After all, he'd broken the last promise he'd made—to love, honor, and protect Mariah. However, he jutted his chin toward Zeke and asked, "What's that?"

"That you'll step away if you feel like you're getting too close."

Now that was a ridiculous request if he'd ever heard one. *Too close.* He liked Ava, but he wasn't foolish enough to do anything to jeopardize her safety.

"I don't think—"

Zeke thrust his palm up, interrupting Zack's counter statement. "Just promise me, man. You know the Bible says something about man making plans in his heart, but God directing his steps."

"Oh, so you're quoting the Bible now?"

"Hey, I'm just saying that you're different, and this situation could turn out in a way you weren't expecting, and if it does, you will remember *why* you're with her in the first place."

Zack bit his tongue. He wasn't sure if he should be offended or not. What was Zeke really trying to say?

"I'm well aware of the job. I've got Ava, and she knows that."

"I'm sure *Ava* does," Zeke said, emphasizing Ava's name.

Why were they even having this conversation?

"So, did you stop by to help me go through this shareholder list, or was there something else?" It was eleven at night. Zack hoped Zeke would have some other plans because the thought of working this late on a Friday evening was usually the last thing on his agenda.

"Neither. I received a notification that someone was in the building. I knew it had to be you. Since I was already out and close by, figured I'd stop in to see what was up with you."

"Usually people send text messages or call when that happens."

"This is a special situation. I think you'd agree." Zeke winked, something he always did when he felt like he'd proven his point.

"See you Monday, man."

Zeke stood. "Okay. Have fun with those records. Let me know if you find anything, but not tonight though. I'm going to bed."

Zack watched his brother disappear on the other side of the entry doors. When the elevator chimed, Zack settled back in front of his laptop screen to resume his task. He sorted the list from the person with the greatest interest in Langston Brands: Philip Hardy. Zack ran his name through their database. While their system crawled, his phone rang. He almost didn't answer it when he thought about Zeke interfering again. But then Ava's image surfaced in his mind.

Without another thought, he pressed the button on his Bluetooth without screening the call.

"Zack," Ava's voice trembled, sending ripples through his entire being.

He jumped to his feet. "What happened?" He hoped his tone didn't cause her more anxiety, but he was certain the worry he felt also laced his voice.

"I think someone came into my house," she whispered, her voice still shaky.

Zack grabbed his car keys and hustled out of his office. "I'm on my way. Tell me exactly what happened."

"After I showered, I came into the kitchen to make a cup of peppermint tea like I do every night before bed. When I picked up the gift bag filled with chocolates, I found the envelope under it. Same envelope and paper as the one my dad showed us last week."

He jogged to his car and hopped in, transitioning the phone to his car's Bluetooth as Ava talked. He had a twenty-minute drive ahead of him, fifteen if he could help it, especially with the lighter traffic at night.

Zack pressed a button, and his engine roared to life. He peeled out of the parking space, not giving a thought to warming the engine as he often did, and navigated his truck onto the open road. He didn't like the idea of someone having the audacity to go into her home. This was an emergency case, which typically resulted in him recommending that his client take advantage of The Four Kings' private apartment facility. But Ava had family. How would she or the rest of the Langstons feel about such an arrangement?

∞

Ava despised the feelings of vulnerability and helplessness she experienced after finding the letter and having to call Zack. She'd always been able to take care of her own personal safety, but recent events casted a shadow of doubt in her mind—dark, crippling, and intimidating—a shadow she didn't like one bit.

Ava paced in front of her living room window, peeping every minute and a half for Zack's truck to pull into her driveway, although she knew he was at least twenty minutes away.

"Will you do me a favor and double check to make sure all of your doors are locked?"

"They're locked, but I'll check again," Ava said. She scurried over to the front door. Locked. Kitchen door that led to the garage. Locked. "All the doors are secured. Did you check to see if the cameras picked up anything on your end?"

"I'll check when I get there. My first thought was to get to you as soon as possible."

Her head, pulse, and heart thumped in synchronization.

"Okay. How is it possible for someone to get in here with all the security we have set up? And how am I supposed to stay in this house knowing someone could get inside and not trigger the alarm system?"

"Ava, listen to my voice." She stopped pacing and focused on the deep, soothing baritone. Her heart rate dipped a little. "Are you with me?"

Ava nodded first, then responded, "Yes."

"We have a solution if you're concerned about staying in your home. That's something we can discuss after I get to you and check things out."

She appreciated that he was calm and focused because she, on the other hand, was filled with the shakes.

"Okay," she said through one long breath. "How much longer will it take you to get to me—I mean, get here?"

"About five more minutes."

"You must be breaking all kinds of traffic laws."

He half-chuckled. "Something like that. Just want to make sure you're okay."

"Thank you. I know this is interrupting your night. You weren't planning to be on night babysitting duty."

"I'm on duty whenever you need me."

That simple statement caused a ripple of semi-romantic emotions—emotions she shouldn't even have for her bodyguard slash private security or whatever he wanted to call himself. *He's getting paid to be here for you,* she had to keep reminding herself.

"Thank you, Zack."

She heard a motor running and ran to peep out of the blinds. He'd made it. Now her heart rate settled just a little bit more.

Ava unlocked and opened the door, poised at the entrance, and waited for Zack. He climbed out of the car and advanced toward her front door wearing that serious look she'd become accustomed to seeing. When they came face-to-face, he lost professionalism and embraced her. He'd moved off instinct, a gesture she was sure he regretted when he pulled away and frowned. She braced herself for an apology that didn't follow. But still, it was on the tip of his tongue. He parted his lips but closed them again.

"You good? Mind if I have a look around?"

Ava stepped to the side and allowed him the freedom to enter her house. "No. Go ahead." She moved on his heels, eyeing the video camera footage he scrolled through, checking windows, doors, and the cameras to see if they'd been tampered with.

After going through each room, they ended up in the kitchen where Ava handed him the note. The lines in his forehead deepened, and his eyebrows and lips were scrunched. His voice was still calm. "Mind if we sit? I want to talk to you about what I think we need to do next."

Ava's heart thumped as she led him to her living room sofa. She sat with one foot tucked under her bottom and pulled one of the fringed decorative pillows to her chest. The silence in the room was a bit unnerving. No TV or music in the background, only the light sounds of their breath.

"So, what now?"

Zack took one look at her, then hunched forward, sending a whiff of his masculine tantalizing scent her way. He put his elbows on his knees and clasped his hands. "The first thing we need to do is get you out of this house. We have two options. The first one is for you to move in with your parents or one of your sisters until this is resolved. The second option is for you to stay in The Four Kings' private facility. It's an apartment-style complex where you'll have your own space and additional security around the clock."

Ava felt like he put more emphasis on her staying at their private complex, but was that even necessary?

She took a deep breath and reached out and touched his arm. He turned his head in her direction, but his body remained forward. "You were hired to protect me, so what do you recommend?"

She saw the answer in his eyes seconds before he answered. "I'd feel more comfortable with you in our facility because someone will always be around to look after you. You'd not only have me but other members of our team. Someone will be posted up outside of your door for the duration of your stay. Our internal security system is top notch because we created it ourselves. I have full confidence in our ability to keep you safe if you stay there, but the choice isn't only mine to make. You have a say in where you want to live. One thing you must consider is that this may take a week or a month to solve. Take that into consideration when making your decision."

"Doesn't sound like I have much of a choice at all."

"You do. You may want to talk to your family about it."

Her parents wouldn't mind the arrangement at all. Anything to keep her safe, they would say. Her sisters could go either way, but seeing as though they weren't equipped like The Four Kings to ensure her safety, staying with them wouldn't be the best choice. What if this cuckoo person decided to add the sister she decided to stay with to their list of vengeance seeking? She couldn't do that to them. The temporary move to The Four Kings' private facility was the best option for now.

"I know exactly what their response would be, which is why I'm going to take you up on the offer to stay in your private facility. I'll give them a call once I'm all moved in."

He didn't say that he was relieved she'd chosen his preferred option, but she could see it in the way his shoulders visibly relaxed a little and the frown lines in his forehead disappeared. He didn't smile though, only nodded. "Okay then. Pack up everything you need, and we'll get you moved in tonight. While you do that, I'll make a call to ensure everything is ready upon your arrival."

"Okay. I'll go pack." Ava stood and trudged through the house into her master bedroom. She removed five dresses and a combination of her favorite slacks and blouses for work. Of course, she needed yoga pants for workouts and to relax in the evenings after leaving the office, pajamas, jeans, and tees. After a while, she turned to face the heap of clothes on her bed. She was packing like she planned to go away forever.

Well, the truth was that they didn't know how long this arrangement would last. However, she opted to stop and fill her suitcases with what she'd pulled out of her closet and drawers so far. If she needed anything more, she could always come back to get it.

Ava stuffed two oversized suitcases with her clothes, hair, body, and makeup products. "This should do it." She didn't really like packing because she always left something. And packing last minute only added to the pressure of ensuring she had everything she needed.

She strolled into the living room where Zack still sat. When he saw her, he stood, but continued his phone conversation. "Yes. Apartment 205 will be perfect. It was cleaned a couple of days ago.... Yes. We'll get Ava's grocery list and have Janine do the shopping.... Thank you.... Yes. Thanks.... Text the code to me.... Bye."

This was really happening. Moving to a private facility because someone thought it a fond idea to play with her life.

Zack collected both rolling suitcases. "Sure you have everything you need?"

"Yeah. I think I'm all good. Whatever I don't have, I can get later."

He turned away from her like a soldier and conducted a final sweep of her house before locking it up. "Okay. follow me."

The seriousness of the situation brought on a throbbing headache, yet Zack's presence and the hope that this move would keep her safe gave her a sense of peace in a situation where she otherwise would have lost her mind.

Chapter Eight

A va wasn't sure what she expected when she agreed to move into The Four Kings' private facility for a short while, but granite countertops, shiny hardwood flooring, and a pillow-top mattress weren't it. The walls were plain—off white with no pictures—which was to be expected. This wasn't anyone's permanent residence. An oversized hanging clock was the extent of any wall decorations.

Ava had partially unpacked last night. With today being a Saturday, she didn't have to worry about going into the office for work. Truthfully, she needed the off time to settle into the space and to recharge. Last night was the best sleep she'd had in the past couple of weeks, and although she felt it, her fitness watch agreed, displaying an *excellent* status for sleep and recharge.

It was after midnight when she'd settled in last night, so she hadn't bothered contacting her sisters. She started a video chat to update them. When they were both logged on, Ava said, "Good morning. How are y'all?"

"Good. Are y'all still planning to meet me for kickboxing at noon?" Layla asked.

Ava massaged her forehead. "I completely forgot."

"I have you plugged into my calendar. I plan to be there. Not going to lunch after though. Marcel and I are hanging out today. We haven't seen each other much this week," Crystal said.

"How'd you forget, Ava? Too busy being protected by Mr. Handsome?" Layla said and laughed. Crystal chuckled, too.

"Something like that." Ava held her phone to show them her surroundings.

"Where are you?" Crystal and Layla both asked.

Ava explained the details of last night, starting from the non-date to how she ended up in The Four Kings' private facility.

"Do you need us to come to you?" Crystal asked.

"No, I'm fine. This place is secure. I'm planning to rest today."

"Rest or hang out with Zack—you know, in a non-date sort of way?" Layla teased.

"Ignore her, Ava," Crystal said, pursing her lips and shaking her head.

"Don't worry. I am."

Crystal continued, "Have there been any updates? Any luck with the shareholder list?"

"From my understanding, they've narrowed it down to five people with the largest interests and are moving from there. Zack mentioned something about conducting background investigations into those names he selected—looking into their financials and things like that. Hopefully, that'll give them some idea of where to start. I'm not certain about his next steps."

"Well, he seems capable, so I'd like to think he knows what he's doing," Crystal said.

"So does this mean you won't be coming into the office next week?" Layla asked.

"I don't think I need to stay locked up in here. I plan to continue with my normal routine and keep my same schedule. But this weekend, I need to rest."

"Well, do you need us to bring you groceries or anything, or has Zack taken care of that, too?" Layla asked, putting way too much emphasis and sweetness on Zack's name.

"See, you're on this call to start mess," Ava started.

"Who me?" Layla asked, her voice raised an octave, pressing a hand into her chest, feigning innocence.

"Yes, you, but since you asked, yes, I have someone who's going to take care of the grocery shopping for me. All I need you two to do right now is pray and keep your eyes open in case you notice anything suspicious. I want this mess over as soon as possible."

"Okay, so now I'm with Layla. Is there anything going on we need to know about? Is this li'l arrangement something he would do for any of his clients, or is it just you because this seems like a lot?"

"Is it really a lot if my life is on the line? And let's not forget he's getting paid to protect me," Ava reminded her sisters, as well as herself.

Crystal nodded. "You do have a point there."

"Well, doesn't sound like you need us at all." Layla playfully pouted. "Crys, I guess we better get ready if we're gonna make it to the kickboxing class on time."

Ava jumped at the sound of someone knocking on her front door. Her breath caught in her chest.

"You okay?" Layla asked.

"Yeah. It's just that someone's at the door."

Who else knew she was there other than Zack?

Her phone vibrated, and a text message from him appeared in her notifications.

Z: Janine is on her way up to get your grocery list.

She released the pent-up air and looked through the peephole. A young, pretty black woman with gorgeous curly hair stood on the other side of the door.

Both her sisters stared into the screen waiting for answers.

"I've gotta go. The lady is here to get my grocery order."

Layla hiked an eyebrow. "*Ummm-hmmm.* Okay then. Be safe, and we'll check in with you later."

"Bye."

Ava ended the call, unlocked the door, and opened it.

The woman smiled wide. Ava immediately noticed features similar to Zack's, mostly her eyes.

"Hey. I'm Janine Kingsland. Did Zack tell you I was coming?"

Ava nodded and looked to the left to see the bodyguard standing watch outside her door. He lifted his chin in a gesture that said Janine was an approved visitor. She certainly felt safe with him standing there. The man looked like he worked out alongside The Rock.

"Yes. Just received a message from him. Come on in." Ava stepped to the side, fully opening the door for Janine to enter.

Janine walked in, sat on the couch, and pulled out her phone like she'd gone through this task hundreds of times.

"So, did Zack explain things to you—that I'll be your contact while you're here? So if you need anything—food, toiletries, dry cleaning, whatever you can think of—reach out to me, and I'll take care of it. Take down my number before we get started on your grocery order."

Ava keyed in Janine's number as she called it out. Saved.

"Alright. Now that we've got that out of the way, let's get you some food in here. Tell me what you like, and I'll add it to the list."

Janine paused, her hand poised over her phone's keypad.

"Okay. In the meantime, I'll order some takeout for breakfast. I'm starving."

She and Janine went through the details of Ava's staple kitchen items. As if she'd summoned him when she spoke about takeout, a message from Zack came through on her cell.

97

Z: On my way with breakfast. Give me five minutes.

This man was almost perfect, wasn't he? Sure. Right now, his sole goal was to ensure she didn't get poisoned again, but would he be as thoughtful in a relationship?

Ava waved her phone in the air. "Well, looks like breakfast—well, brunch—is taken care of. Zack is on his way up with food."

Janine hiked an eyebrow, which made Ava think she'd done something wrong.

"Is everything okay?"

"Seems like it's more than okay. My cousin is doing quite the job taking care of you."

What was that supposed to mean? Ava couldn't be certain she even wanted to know, but Janine's comment had her curious. Her curiosity held her mind captive as they walked through the list of grocery items Ava wanted to order.

Seconds later, there were a few light taps on her front door, which could only mean Zack had arrived.

"I'll get it." Ava jumped to her feet. "Zack's here, and I didn't realize how hungry I am until now."

Ava answered the door and relieved Zack of the tray of coffee cups. The dark circles around his eyes screamed lack of sleep. He may have needed the cup of coffee more than her.

She waltzed over to the sofa where Janine sat and handed her a cup. "Looks like there's one for you, too, with your name on it."

"Deluxe service. Kings' service for a queen," Janine said, her eyes locked on Zack, who seemed to be purposely ignoring whatever message she tried to send. He kept his attention on Ava and trailed her into the kitchen.

"Janine, please excuse Ava for just a minute."

Janine didn't respond, only pursed her lips in such a way as to make Ava think she was about to say something sassy to the effect of *ummm-hmmm.*

Zack's eyes pierced hers, almost convincing Ava that he cared beyond his duty. "Are you good? How'd you sleep?"

Ava sipped her coffee and moaned. "Yum. This is good." She lifted the cup in a toast. Skinny caramel macchiato with extra foam. "I slept well. Honestly, better than I have since this whole thing started."

"That means you're comfortable, which is what I hoped. You're safe here. If at any time you can't reach me, you can call Janine."

Ava nodded and peered around his shoulder at Janine, who was focused on both Ava and Zack.

"Thanks. Your timing is almost perfect. I'd just mentioned that I would order takeout, and here you are, saving the day again."

"Good at his job, huh?" Janine called across the room, inserting herself into the conversation. She smirked, and Ava could sense Janine was doing some type of familial teasing.

"I'll get out of your way. I ordered that veggie omelet you mentioned you liked, along with a blueberry pancake." Zack tapped the bag and set it on the counter. He jutted his thumb toward the door. "I'm gonna get to work and let you and Janine finish up."

"Oh, I thought you were gonna stay and eat with me—keep me company and catch me up on the case," Ava added for good measure because of Janine's attentive eyes and ears. She probably assumed something was going on between them.

And that couldn't be farther from the truth.

∞

Janine was clearly making a big deal out of something that wasn't. There was nothing happening between him and Ava. He'd give the same service to anyone. And he had. Before he chained himself to his desk, prior to Mariah's passing, his last client stayed in The Four Kings' private facility when they'd only owned a duplex.

However, he obviously had a difficult time turning down any request Ava made. Dining with her had been like fresh air to his lungs and something he'd grown accustomed to in this small amount of time. Had it been the same for her? Was that why she thought he'd stay?

"I didn't want to overcrowd you. I figured you needed your rest after last night."

"I do. And I plan on resting." She opened the food container. "But this pancake is even made for two—or three," she added when Janine gave one of her inquisitive looks. Eyebrows shifting high on her forehead. Eyes widening like she'd discovered some hidden truth. "I don't mind sharing with you two. I know I won't eat it all by myself." Ava motioned to find plates in the cupboard without waiting for a response from him or Janine.

She washed her hands and sliced the pancake in three pieces, handing a plate and fork to them both.

"Trust me. The coffee is even better with it," Ava said and took her first bite.

Janine mouthed to him, "I like her."

Zack shook his head and bit into his own fluffy piece of sweet goodness. He hadn't been remotely interested in anyone since Mariah died, so he could understand the unwarranted excitement or questions going through Janine's head. However, she was far off base in this case.

"So, Janine, how did you come to work with The Four Kings?"

"Nepotism," Zack answered.

Janine burst into laughter.

"Yeah, he might be right, but I pull my weight around the office. I work hard, even on the weekend. Look at me. I'm taking care of our precious clients, just like my cousins taught me."

"She's good help. Even though she got the job unfairly, we appreciate her around the office."

"You ever thought about doing the kind of work Zack does? More security work?"

"It's crossed my mind a time or two, but right now I think I'm in a good place looking after Zack, Zeke, and the twins.

Someone has to do it, and I don't know if anyone else can tolerate them and get them in line like I can."

Zack tossed his head back and laughed. His brothers may be a problem from time to time, but not him.

"Zack is a good one though. The responsible one. The leader. Strait-laced. It's nice seeing him happy again."

Ava's gaze locked on him, expecting more of an explanation. He tilted his head in warning to Janine. She was talking too much. And about what? Where was this coming from? He wasn't any different today than when he started this assignment a few weeks ago.

Apparently she took the hint because she gulped down the remainder of her pancake and asked, "Ava, is there anything else we need to add to the list?" She read the current items off to her.

Ava added strawberries and blueberries. "I think that's all."

"What about nuts to snack on like peanuts, almonds, or cashews?"

"Please, no nuts, unless you want to find me passed out on the floor. I have a peanut and tree nut allergy."

Janine sucked air between her teeth and shook her head. "We definitely don't want that."

Zack shot her a serious look. "Do you have a spare EpiPen? I'll need that."

He could never be too careful, though he was certain Ava knew to stay away from nut products. Based on their current predicament, it wasn't unlikely that the person working to harm her could come across the information and use it to finish the job.

Ava hesitated as if to question if he wanted her to get the device now. But Zack hadn't budged or taken his eyes off her. That should be enough to convey his seriousness.

She finally stood. "Let me get it for you."

Ava returned to the room and handed over the device to him. He only nodded and slid the EpiPen inside jacket pocket. The muscles in his body were now relaxed.

Janine looked between the two of them, stood and slipped her crossbody purse over her head and shoulder. "I'm going to run a few errands for myself, pick up your groceries, and stop by later. If you think of something to add to your list before I get back, send me a text."

"Thanks, Janine. I will."

"Is there anything else the two of you need me to do?" she asked, though she'd already started inching toward the door.

"That's all for me," Ava said.

"I don't have anything, but if something comes up, I'll give you a call."

"Okay. Enjoy the rest of your afternoon, and I'll see you all later."

The clicking of the doorknob signaled they were alone again. Signaled his mind to focus on anything but the beautiful woman in front of him. Janine had made it awkward for him and probably for

Ava, too, attempting to point out things that didn't exist between them.

"So, are you working when you leave here? You look like you could use some rest."

Zack rubbed the shadow under his chin. "I haven't been to sleep yet, so I may shut my eyes for a few hours after leaving here, then I'm out to check out my first guy."

"Oh, what do you mean by check him out? What do you know about him so far?"

"Philip Harper is a thirty-six-year-old techie who owns his own IT consulting firm. Within the last year, he invested in Langston Brands' stock, which makes up the largest amount of his portfolio. He is an oversharer on social media—documents all of his hangout spots by checking in and adding photos."

"So what are you planning to do?"

"He'll be at the gallery opening of his cousin in downtown Houston tonight. We'll have a chance meeting there."

"I want in on this."

"Absolutely not. If he's our guy, and he sees me with you, he would never engage me in conversation—at least if he's smart, he wouldn't."

"Couldn't I wear a wig or something?"

Zack chuckled. "Nope. You're staying here. Safe. But I'll keep you posted on the outcome."

Sure, she'd probably grow tired of being in that apartment alone, but hanging out in the open with him while he planned to make contact with a possible suspect was definitely not something Ava should be doing.

"Okay. Thanks. I guess I couldn't ask for more than that."

"Right." Zack stood, and Ava followed suit. "I'd better get going so that I can get that sleep you said I desperately need because you can see the knapsacks under my eyes."

Ava tossed her head back and laughed. Her curls dangled behind her head. Zack fought the urge to reach out to feel how soft her hair was. That was his cue to get out of the apartment. Fast. He was clearly sleep deprived.

"I did not say that. But sleep will do you some good since you haven't slept all night." A beat later, she added, "I'll take your trash."

Ava took both their plates and disappeared into the kitchen to empty the scraps. When she returned, Zack stood at the door with his hand on the knob. He had to get out of there before he did something his rested self wouldn't do. Ava closed the distance between them.

"Thanks for everything, Zack. I know this is what you're paid to do, but it's worth me saying that I appreciate you being good at your job."

Zack rubbed his hands along her shoulders. "You're welcome. You're in good hands." Hands that he snatched away from her skin like he'd touched fire. Mixed emotions played through her eyes. Confusion. Content. Maybe even pleasure.

He shouldn't have touched her like that. He'd crossed the line with Ava.

Again.

"I'll be in touch," he said and ran out of the apartment like he'd gotten caught stealing.

Though he wasn't the thief in this situation. It was Ava who was unknowingly stealing something from him that he didn't realize was still operational after Mariah.

His heart.

Chapter Nine

A rt wasn't his thing. And neither were the sounds of the soft jazz music playing through the sound system. A couple of hours in the tux, and Zack was already missing his leather jacket. He tugged at the tie around his neck as he strolled through the crowd of spectators, eavesdropping on conversations here and there. He heard talk of everything from how talented the artist was to discussions that speculated the artist's parents' money and reputation were the only reason he'd been afforded the opportunity to showcase his work tonight. That was nothing new. There would always be someone who couldn't seem to be happy for another person's success. He shrugged and continued his stroll, stopping to gaze at an oversized black canvas painting with a short diagonal stroke of white paint in the center, boasting a price tag of two thousand dollars.

Who in their right mind would even consider wasting money on this?

"Beautiful, isn't it?"

Zack turned and came face-to-face with a pair of green eyes, special thanks to colored contact lenses. The woman's hair was braided into a high ponytail, accentuating her cheekbones. Her black spaghetti-strapped dress hugged every curve she had. Zack raised an eyebrow, waiting for her to correct or at least explain herself.

"*Beautiful* isn't quite the word I'd use to describe it."

"I take it you're not that into art." She looked him over. "You're not married—at least you're not wearing a ring—and you're here alone. So, why are you here? The music?"

"I like to try new things every now and again. Can't say you don't like something if you've never given it a shot, right?"

"I can agree with that. Come, walk with me. Let's see if we can find some art you may like."

He didn't want to walk with the woman, but he didn't have a plausible reason to say no. Besides, there weren't many people alone tonight, and walking alongside her wouldn't make him stand out.

"I'm Tanya, by the way," she said and jutted her hand toward him.

He shook it. All that could come to mind was that touching her hand didn't elicit the same stirrings within him like it did when he touched Ava's hand. Every single time.

He stuffed both hands into his pockets and strolled with her. "I'm Zack. Nice to meet you, Tanya. So, do you come to art shows often?"

"Yeah. It's sort of my thing. I'm an artist."

"Really? So, what do you think of this?" Zack stopped in front of another art piece that he'd consider relatively plain.

Elementary even. But he wasn't an artist and apparently didn't know a good piece when he saw it, especially if that black-and-white piece was considered beautiful. He peered over his shoulder to see another group standing and gawking at the canvas. Zack shook his head.

"See, you have to understand the strokes. To some people, this may look like an ordinary sunset of some sort, but within this abstract painting, I can feel the artist's pain just by paying attention to the strokes." She reached out and ran her fingers along the painting. Nope. He saw nothing but a canvas of what looked like what some amateur did during a bring-your-own-bottle paint night. But perhaps he wasn't supposed to understand, and that wasn't why he was there in the first place.

"Sorry. I don't see it."

She laughed. "It's okay. Most won't. Let's try another one."

Tanya sashayed across the room to the next piece, which happened to be the best one he'd seen so far. It was an image of a woman painted nude. She was painted from the profile angle, with her legs crossed, looking over her shoulder. The most captivating thing about the image was her eyes. They looked alive in a way he couldn't explain.

"I take it you like this one."

"I do."

"I'd say this is probably Gabriel the Slayer's best work," a male voice said.

The man walked up and stood on Zack's left.

Zack turned to match the voice with the face. Recognition registered in his mind. Just the man he was hoping to see. Philip Harper. The man wore red shades with a matching button-down shirt and a suit jacket that appeared two sizes too small with a pair of skinny jeans. Based on appearances, Zack wouldn't peg him as the guy responsible for what was happening to Ava, but judging a book by its cover was what got most people in trouble.

The Slayer? "Do you follow all of his work?" Zack asked.

"Something like that," Philip said and folded his arms across his chest. "I'm more of an investor in finer things."

"Such as art?"

"I collect a few pieces here and there, but only to sell later. So yeah, an investor mostly. If it doesn't make money, it doesn't make sense, right?" He offered a half-hearted chuckle before adding, "Isn't that the saying?"

Tanya tapped his shoulder and whispered her good-bye, apparently not keen on the fact that he'd given his full attention to Mr. Philip. Zack nodded, and she walked away. He returned his attention to Philip.

Philip ticked off on his fingers. "Art, stocks, real estate. I dabble in a little of everything." True to the persona he presented on social media, the man didn't mind talking about himself.

Zack extended his palm and shook Philip's hand. "I'm Zack."

"I'm Philip Harper. Pleased to meet you. So, are you looking for any investment opportunities?"

"Depends. Do you have any opportunities or tips?"

Zack pulled out his phone, hoping that Philip would do the same. That would be his chance to use their firm-developed software to tap into Philip's phone, gather his location history information, and track him going forward.

Philip released an overly exaggerated sigh. Zack could feel the man's breath and smell what he'd eaten for dinner. He took a step back. "Ordinarily, I'd give advice, but not today. I'm still trying to figure out what to do about my Langston Brands stock. I invested a big chunk of money in that company. The value is tanking, and I can't decide whether to throw in the towel and take my losses or hold to see if it turns around. Things always turn around, but I don't know if I want to wait. Shouldn't have listened to my ex-girlfriend and bought the stock. Wouldn't be in this situation—losing my money and such."

"You seem like the kind of guy who doesn't mind a little risk, and you didn't invest everything in Langston Brands. I'm sure you can recoup your losses in other ways."

Zack watched Philip's body language—paying attention to everything a person didn't say was equally as important as listening to what came out of their mouth. The man stiffened, and he cocked his head to the side and squinted at Zack like he was privy to information he hadn't shared. And he was. Zack completed a thorough background check on the man, but Philip wouldn't know that, no matter how techie he was.

Philip finally shrugged and whipped out his phone. His fingers flew across the screen, responding to a text message. Zack only needed Philip's phone to be unlocked for thirty seconds to get what he needed. "While I don't mind risks, like most people, I hate losing money, especially when it's a situation that can be prevented. But anyway, I don't want to get upset in here. Enough about that." Philip gave Zack a once-over and tapped him on the shoulder with his free hand. "You look like you know a thing or two. Maybe I should be asking you for advice."

"Investing is not really my expertise. Art either. My girlfriend loves art, so I figured I'd surprise her with something to add to her collection. That's the only reason I'm here." Ava wasn't his girlfriend, and he was hoping to find something for her this evening, just not art. Answers.

Philip nodded and sent another text.

Zack looked at his phone. Their software had done its job. Mission accomplished.

"Well, I think she'd like this piece. Like I said, it's his best that I've seen, and I should know, he's my cousin." After a beat of silence, he added, "Good luck."

Philip moved across the room to another painting and engaged the group observing the red canvas with two black tattered roses mirroring each other. Zack shrugged and shook his head. He'd never understand.

Zack crossed the gallery in the opposite direction, hoping not to run into Tanya again. And he'd talked enough to Philip for now, gathering the information he needed from his location history. He would investigate it later. Zack didn't get the vibe that he'd harm anyone, but as an investor, Philip didn't tolerate losses well, and that gave Zack pause. Losses came with the territory. Philip should know that more than anyone.

After spending a few minutes pretending to admire the canvas painting of a meadow, something he'd swear he'd seen at his local big box home goods retailer, he eased out of the building and back to his car.

It was time to see Ava again.

∞

Ava had been in The Four Kings' private facility less than twenty-four hours, and she'd already become restless. She'd taken a nap, received her groceries from Janine, talked to her sisters again, and now she was not so patiently waiting for Zack to come back with information about his first suspect. If he was their guy, this would all be over.

She reclined on the sofa, scanning her streaming service app for something to binge watch. Her phone vibrated, and she flipped it over. Ava tossed the remote to the sofa and pressed the green button to answer her dad's video call. Crystal and Layla were already patched in. The light in all their eyes dimmed, and none of them wore a smile like they did most of the time. Ava's stomach did the hokey pokey where it turned itself around, then flipped, dipped, and skipped in her midsection.

"Oh no, what happened?" Ava asked.

Crystal spoke up. "The rumors are true, Ava—at least with our manufacturing operations in Cambodia."

"I don't understand. How could something like this happen and none of us know anything about it?"

"That's exactly what we intend to find out," Layla said.

Crystal nodded in agreement.

The queasiness in Ava's stomach made itself at home. "We have to get in front of this—control the narrative and fix the situation. I'm going out there."

"You need to stay right where you are, safe under the protection of The Four Kings. I'm going. I'm the CEO, so it's my job to handle this."

"Crystal, you being CEO is exactly the reason you need to stay here. Continue working on your image. I should go, especially since I'm the one in charge of meeting with potential buyers. I want to be able to tell Ms. Wertheimer that I've personally looked into it, and we're taking care of the situation." Ava needed to do this. She had to be the one to help dig her family out of this mess and secure the deal with Ms. Wertheimer. Maybe being away would help keep her safe. There's no way the threat could follow her out of the country, right?

Crystal's jaw twitched. All eyes were on her for her approval.

"Dad, do you have any objections to Ava traveling and continuing on this trip with you and Mom?"

"I do not, but what I want to know is what your plan will be once you get here," he said.

"We have no choice but to halt production until we can change the working conditions. If we have to, we'll purchase a new space or continue operations in a temporary facility that is better suited for our employees," Crystal interjected. With Crystal being the CEO, Ava didn't mind her plan. Ultimately, the responsibility would all fall on her shoulders anyway, although all three sisters ran the company.

"I'm no accountant, but that sounds costly," Layla piped in.

"It's a cost we have to bear. We'd lose a lot more if we don't," Crystal said.

"Okay, then it's settled. I'll hold a meeting with our employees there on your behalf. You can even conference in via video if you need to, but we have to take care of it," Ava said *we* meaning *I*. She needed to feel like she was helping the situation in some way instead of being stowed away in a private facility.

Crystal, Layla, and her father all nodded and simultaneously said, "Agreed."

"Ava, I don't mind you going in my place as long as Zack agrees to accompany you to ensure your safety."

Ava started to protest, but Crystal cut her off.

"I'm serious, Ava. We don't want anything happening to you, and since we don't know who's behind the threats on your life, we can't take any chances. Zack goes or you stay."

How could she explain in a way they would understand that being near Zack awakened something within her? Truth was, she couldn't. The chemistry between the two of them wasn't quite something she understood or even experienced before in her life. And she was convinced it wasn't one-sided. He fought it because he was around to protect her—and something else that he hadn't divulged. Maybe he was a private person. She hadn't quite figured him out yet.

But did she even want to?

And what difference would it make?

He was there to do a job. And although she didn't think it was a good idea to travel with him—the more time they spent together, the harder it would be for her to fight her growing attraction to him—there was no one else she felt safer with.

"You're right. Zack needs to come with me. I'll talk with him about it. I'm expecting him in a few minutes." Ava further explained where Zack was in his investigation and where he'd gone this evening.

Ava then directed her attention to Layla. "I guess it's settled—unless Layla has any bad feelings or premonitions about me going."

"Stop trying to be funny. One day, y'all are going to believe me and trust that my premonitions are right." She leaned forward and whispered like that would keep everyone else from hearing her. "Wanna know what my premonitions are about you and Zack?"

Finally, Crystal cracked a smile, and their father cocked an eyebrow.

"Never mind her, Dad. I'm not playing with Layla this evening. How's Mom?"

"She's okay. Resting now. I think seeing the working conditions really broke her heart. She's been sick about it since we saw it for ourselves."

"Give her our love," Layla said, "and have her call me when she wakes up. At least she likes hearing about my premonitions."

Zack's text popped up across her screen.

Be up in five minutes.

"Gotta run. Zack's here. I'll keep you guys posted."

Everyone said their round of good-byes, and Ava left the group call. She ran to the restroom to check her reflection and reapplied lipstick.

What am I even doing?

Three taps on the door, and her stomach fluttered. Looked like her body needed a reminder that she and Zack could be no more than what they currently were. Private security guard and client. Protector and protectee. Nothing more.

Ava glided across the room and opened the door to see Zack standing there in a black tuxedo. She couldn't hide the smile that formed on her lips. She thought he was handsome in the leather jacket, but she was seconds from turning into a puddle at the sight of him in the tuxedo.

"So, you do own something other than that trusty leather jacket," Ava teased and stepped aside to allow him into the apartment.

Zack threw his head back, and a guttural laugh escaped his lips. "So, you've got jokes."

Ava joined him in laughter. When she recovered, she added, "No, not a joke. You know you wear that leather jacket all the time. Probably to bed, too."

Zack laughed some more. After the moment passed, the smile settled on his lips for a moment longer. And she thought her stomach and heart would play patty cake.

Ava cleared her throat and sat on one end of the sofa while Zack sat on the opposite end.

"So first, tell me about tonight. What did you find out? And do you think he's our guy?"

Zack shared the details of the evening with her, including his meeting a woman named Tanya. That part he could have kept to himself because she found herself a little jealous. Ava shook her head to rid herself of the thoughts. *He's not my man. What is wrong with me? Get it together, Ava.*

"Okay, so what are the next steps? Do you just move on to the next person or what?"

"Well, first, we're going to examine his location history to see if he was anywhere near you on any of the occasions where you had the incidents, then, depending on what we find, we'll move on to the next person."

"What does your gut tell you about him? Do you think this Philip guy might be our person?"

Zack shook his head. "I'm not quite sure yet, to be honest. I'm not entirely convinced it's him, but I don't think we should dismiss him just yet."

Ava didn't get any assurance from that. All she heard was that this would likely not be over as soon as she'd like.

"Okay. Thanks for the update."

"You're welcome. My goal is to keep open communication between us."

"I have an update of my own."

Zack slid to the edge of the sofa and rested his forearms on his knees. "Okay. Go ahead."

"The rumors about the sweatshop are true, and I'm traveling to Cambodia to help fix it."

"You're absolutely not."

Chapter Ten

D id Ava not understand the potential exposure she'd be subjecting herself to if she traveled out of the country? Albeit, the threats could be localized, but one could never be certain in situations like this. And he wouldn't let Ava out of his sight in such a way that her fate would end up the same as Mariah's.

Her eyelids fluttered, and she rolled her neck. His response had obviously upset her, so he braced himself for her pushback.

"What do you mean, absolutely not? My family's company is on the line, and you expect me not to do anything about it?"

"And your life is on the line. How do you propose I protect you if you're thousands of miles away? I won't allow anything to happen to you, Ava. Not like…" Zack caught himself before he said too much. Ava didn't need to know the full details of how he failed his wife. And she was now dead because of him.

Her gaze softened, and she looked and waited to hear more, but he didn't want to talk about it.

"I know you can't protect me if I'm out of the country without you, so the idea is for you to come with me. I've already talked to my dad. He's okay with it and whatever extra fees your firm has to charge." She closed the space between them and placed a soft touch on his bicep. Honestly—and shamefully—she'd already convinced him with that one gesture. Not the extra money. Not the fact that she'd talked to her father about this, and he'd given his approval. It was her touch and the way it made him experience emotions he hadn't even experienced with Mariah, and he loved her with every fiber of his being. *This can't be good.*

How was he supposed to get through the rest of this gig, especially traveling out of the country with her?

Zack released a heavy breath. "Okay. I understand, but I'll need a few days to coordinate our travel arrangements and secure another member of our team who will serve as my backup and to stand guard outside your hotel room door. The Four Kings will make the travel arrangements. First class."

Apparently satisfied with his response, her posture softened. "I half-expected you to say The Four Kings has a private jet or something. Not that you'd need it in a situation like this."

"As a matter of fact, we're in the process of purchasing one."

"Seriously?"

"You seem surprised."

"I am, but I suppose I shouldn't be surprised considering you all have your own private building. What else do I not know about The Four Kings?"

Zack shrugged. "Not much else to tell. Just a family of brothers who own and operate a private security firm."

Ava made herself comfortable on the couch, tucking one foot beneath her, stretching her arm over the back of the sofa and resting her cheek against the back of her hand. "Private security firm. Private residential facilities. And private jets. How did all of this come about, if you don't mind my asking?"

Zack relaxed against the back of the sofa, tugged, and loosened his tie. Some of his fondest and most frustrating memories were centered around the start of their business. He and his brothers had always been close growing up. Their father ensured his sons had a bond, stating that their bond was what would make them a force in this world. Make them strong. Relentless. And give them the ability to accomplish anything they set their minds to.

"All three of my brothers are ex-military. Zeke is the oldest. He retired from the army with twenty-one years of service and went to join his mentor's security firm. It didn't take him long to figure out that he didn't like the way the man did business, and he suggested we start The Four Kings. The rest of us liked the idea and jumped on board. I left Houston Police Department, and the twins left the military. They weren't eligible for retirement, but were ready for something different. And here we are. Because of Zeke's military background, we've secured large government contracts and provided services for politicians and celebrities."

"And that's how y'all became rich?"

Zack chuckled.

"I wouldn't call it rich. Just comfortable. We're wise with the way we conduct business." He didn't think it necessary to add that their first contract was a million-dollar one.

"A private jet is far from comfortable."

"I'm not downplaying it. We've definitely done well for ourselves, but it's because we're stronger together, which I imagine is the same thing behind Langston Brands. Your family is working together, so your business is successful."

Ava gave a slow nod. "I guess you're right. Once both of my sisters and I were on board, the business thrived more than it had in the past. We're certainly not done yet. Once we can get past this situation, we can continue moving in an upward direction."

"You will."

"So, the twins… What are their names?"

"Jake and Joshua."

"I always thought it would be cool to have younger twin siblings. I can remember back when I was a kid, asking my mom to have twins, but I got something better in Crystal and Layla. Since we are so close together in age, it's almost like we're triplets. Like you and your brothers, my sisters and I are close. I'd give my life for them. And I can tell by the way you talk about your brothers that you'd do the same. I like that about you."

Zack hiked an eyebrow.

"What I mean is that your protectiveness is a good trait to have, and it makes you good at your job. I trust you, and I couldn't go on this trip to Cambodia without you."

By this time, Zack had shifted on the sofa so that he faced her with his arm resting across the back of it. Far more comfortable than he should be right now. He'd locked eyes with her and found it hard to look away. "Thank you for that. Knowing you trust me makes protecting you a little easier."

What made it difficult was this *thing* between them. The best course of action was probably to withdraw himself and have Zeke take over—or even Jake or Josh. But he didn't want to leave her hanging like that, especially since she trusted him and they'd developed a positive working relationship.

When the urge to reach out and caress her hand came over him, that was his signal to get out of that apartment as fast as he could. He could only spend small bouts of time with her. How would he get through an entire trip, especially a flight that lasted longer than the recommended number of hours of sleep?

"Unless you need anything else, I'm going to head out."

Ava didn't move from her position on the sofa. Her eyes were zoned in on him. Ordinarily, that would make him uncomfortable, but he sort of liked it. Zack ran an open palm over his face. He had to get it together. Keep it professional. And just do his job. It wasn't a difficult task.

"Are you going to rest or work? You've had a long twenty-four hours. You should probably go with the former."

"As long as I have enough sleep to function, I'm all good. My priority right now is you...and your safety." When had he become sloppy with his words? Maybe he needed more sleep than he thought.

"I appreciate everything you're doing for me. When will you have the details on our travel arrangements?"

"A couple of days. I'll be in touch tomorrow just to keep the lines of communication open."

Zack stood, and Ava followed.

"Sounds good. I'll also get an itinerary to you tomorrow of the places I need to visit."

"The sooner you can get that info to me, the better. It'll help me with the planning we need to do on our end."

Zack strolled to the door.

"Have a good night, and be sure to lock the door behind me. Jax is in the hall if you need anything before I can get back to you."

"Duly noted." Ava saluted him. "Be safe, and have a good night."

Zack nodded and closed the door behind him. When he heard the locks engage, he spent a couple of minutes talking to Jax, the bodyguard outside Ava's door, about anything he may have noticed out of the ordinary. Satisfied that everything was going well, he left the complex to head home.

He'd thought for a moment to go to the office, but he didn't need to go in just to check Philip's location history. That could be done from the confines of his house. Ava's assessment had been spot-on. He needed rest, but lately his dreams had been centered around her. At least awake, he could force himself to focus on her case or something entirely different. He had no control over his dreams.

The best thing for him to do was concentrate on what he could control—getting answers so he could keep her safe.

∞

Instead of going into Langston Brands' headquarters Monday morning, Ava visited The Four Kings' office. After talking with Zack last night, they thought it would be helpful if she could get a glimpse into their operations to further provide her more comfort, which she didn't necessarily need, but to also bring her into their logistics meeting for their upcoming travel.

Before Zack mentioned The Four Kings would soon purchase a private jet, she'd imagined them working out of a tiny facility with a small office space for each brother, and file cabinets taking up most of the room in each of their designated offices—something like what she'd seen on TV shows and movies.

Janine greeted Ava when she entered through the wooden double entry doors, which gave off castle-like vibes. She rounded her receptionist desk and extended her hand. "Good to see you again, Ava. Can I get you a bottled water, coffee, or tea?"

"Bottled water would be fine."

"I'll take you to the conference room and bring you that water. Zack and Zeke are waiting for you."

Ava's pumps clicked against the hardwood floors just like those in her temporary apartment as she followed Janine down a long corridor to the conference room. Unlike Langston Brands' office space, The Four Kings' facility didn't have cubicles. Instead, rows of connected desks with oversized screens filled the area. Privacy screen filters covered the monitors. She learned that was the cyber security area. Large screens covered the walls littered with information she couldn't even begin to decipher.

Once they passed that area, Janine stopped at the first door to the left, double-tapped, and walked inside, announcing, "I've got the package."

"Thanks, Janine," Zack said, shaking his head at her reference to Ava.

Ava looked at Janine and smirked. With the heaviness of their jobs, Janine seemed to be the one who kept the atmosphere light.

As for Zack, he was clearly back in his comfort zone, wearing his leather jacket, hovering over the conference table next to a man who could be his identical twin. Same smooth toffee skin, bald head, impressive jawline, and lean, muscular build. Opposite Zack, he was dressed more formally in a white button-down dress shirt, red tie, and slacks.

"I'm Zeke Kingsland, the brains of this operation."

Ava chuckled.

"Everyone knows that if you're the brains of the operation, you don't have to say it," Zack said.

Zeke reached out and shook her hand. The man was a complete replica of Zack, except he looked to be a few years older, as Zack mentioned, and his gaze and touch didn't cause everything within her to quake.

"It's nice to meet you, Zeke. Thank you for everything your firm is doing to protect me."

"You're welcome. I guess that means my brother is doing a pretty good job." He glanced at Zack, and they had an unspoken conversation with their eyes.

"I trust him with my life," Ava said to Zeke, but her gaze was honed in on Zack. She could just melt from the way the man's eyes made her feel every time he focused on her. One side of his mouth tilted upward, and a shiver crawled up her spine.

"Good to know. Makes his job easier."

Janine returned with a bottled water, handed it to her, and eased back out of the door, shutting it behind her.

"Now that you're here, we can get started," Zack announced. He waved his hand over the conference table, and it came to life. A giant computer was what she'd call it. Touchscreen. Probably somewhere between sixty to eighty inches and straight from a movie screen. Ava's mouth dropped open.

Zeke's chest puffed. He covered his fist with a palm and stood poised to give her an explanation of what she was looking at. "We call it The Kings' Table—an exclusive oversized technical device, much like a computer that allows us to work cohesively as a team, examine data, and solve security problems. It is an internally developed software that cannot be hacked from the outside. A hacker would have to stand in this room to crack our system."

"Just wow." Ava stepped forward and stood next to Zack to get a closer look. He had two maps pulled up on the screen. Both were satellite views of the area they were traveling to, zoomed in and zoomed out.

"So here is where we'll be staying." Zack pointed to the map. "We've already made the reservations where our team will be the only ones with access to the top level. Because what is most important, Ava?"

Would she ever get tired of the vibrations coming from his throat when he said her name? Perhaps Zeke should do the talking from now on.

"My safety," she answered like an elementary student giving an answer to a question her teacher asked repeatedly.

"Right. We have to treat this threat as if it's plausible, even out of the country. And I know you have a job to do when we travel, but I need you to remember that so do I."

Zack informed her that Jax, the bodyguard who was currently detailed to stand guard outside of her door, would travel with them. He'd also stand guard outside of her hotel room door and serve as Zack's backup. He and Zeke discussed access points and travel protocol.

"And this is for you." Zack handed her a cell phone. "This is the only phone you'll use when we travel. In fact, please turn off your personal cell phone and leave it here in Houston. We haven't found any indication that your phone is being tracked or bugged, but let's err on the side of caution. Are you with me?"

He should focus on his choice of words.

Ava nodded. "Yes. Understood."

"Last chance to stay home, Ava. Otherwise, you're going to be seeing much more of that mug than you bargained for," Zeke teased.

At least it's a handsome face.

Ava chuckled. "Zack is good company. If anything, you may want to make sure he has extra backup having to deal with me."

Zeke popped a stick of gum into his mouth and gestured to Zack. Choking back laughter, Zeke asked, "Is that true, brother? Do you need extra backup? Is Miss Langston too much for you to handle?"

He obviously found the idea hilarious.

"If more manpower is what you think we need, then by all means, add someone else to the team. Her safety is all I care about. You two aren't going to rope me into whatever this is. Ava can have whatever she wants. You, too, Mr. Brains of this Operation."

Dang it. *Whatever I want. Does that include you?*

Clearly, she needed to go on a date with someone else so she could flush this man from her system.

Zack and Zeke exchanged looks, a silent conversation happening between the two of them again.

"I think we're all good with Jax," Zeke said, his demeanor back to being serious.

Zack turned to Ava. "I reviewed the itinerary you sent to my e-mail." He tapped across the screen, and seconds later, the locations listed in her message were identified on the maps as red dots. He'd already planned the driving route to each location and identified street cameras.

She knew she probably shouldn't make a joke out of a serious situation like this, but she couldn't help herself. "Looks like someone missed their calling to be a travel agent."

Surprisingly, both Zack and Zeke laughed. Zack stood from his hovering position over the table, and for the first time, she noticed his gun strapped inside of a holster.

Ava sobered, her attention drawn to the weapon on his hip. Zack and Zeke's eyes followed hers.

"Yes, it's necessary, and I'll have it when we travel." He answered her unasked question. "We don't know what we're walking into, especially considering your company is operating a sweatshop. The employees could riot or protest, or any civil disturbance can break out putting you in danger. You just need to be aware it could happen. I don't want you to worry. I've got you."

The authority in his voice would have persuaded her if she wasn't already convinced.

"If there's nothing else, see you tomorrow morning at o-seven hundred hours."

"No. That's all for me."

"Alright then. I'll see to it that you get back to the apartment safely. Jax will meet us there."

Zack wrapped up their meeting with final instructions for tomorrow's takeoff. He'd pick her up, and they'd ride to the airport together along with his backup personnel, Jax. Ava said her good-byes to Zeke and followed Zack out of the conference room. His words, *I've got you,* echoed in her mind.

How was she going to get through a seven-day—or possibly longer—trip with this man and keep her head on straight?

Chapter Eleven

True to his word, Zack arrived at Ava's apartment door ten minutes before seven o'clock. Before knocking on the door, he stopped to talk with Jax.

"Hey, Jax. How was the rest of the evening?" That was sort of a crazy question because if anything unusual had happened, Jax would have reached out. Still didn't hurt to check though.

"Quiet. This may be the easiest job I've ever done."

"That's a good thing, but we don't want to get too relaxed."

Jax checked his watch. "Agreed. About ready to head out?"

"Yes. Ava should be good to go. I texted her before I left, and she said she was just about ready." Zack knocked on the door. "We'll be right out."

Ava flung open the door. Dressed in something as simple as a black track jacket and matching yoga pants, yet she even made that ensemble look good. He was tempted to complain about having someone like her as a client. Sure, he'd worked with attractive women before now, but no one had ever stirred anything in him like Mariah did.

Until Ava.

133

Lord, help me maintain my professionalism throughout this trip. Because everything about Ava tested him every step of the way.

Ava pointed to two large pink hard-cased rolling suitcases. "I'm ready."

"Good thing I didn't pack as heavy. We should've discussed luggage limitations. Woman, is there something you aren't telling me? Are you planning to stay?"

Ava erupted into laughter. "You're being a little dramatic, don't you think? Just clothes, shoes, toiletries, and makeup. The basics."

Whatever it takes to keep you looking like that, a part of him wanted to say. Instead, he said, "Whatever you need. I'll grab those."

Zack stepped into the apartment, grabbed the rolling suitcases, and walked back out, with Ava following.

"Good morning, Jax," she said. "Need a water or bathroom break before we head out?"

He flipped his wrist to check the time. "Two minutes before seven. Yes, I'll take both, and I'll be quick about it."

She stepped to the side to allow him entry, then scuffled into the kitchen to grab a water bottle for him, returning to Zack's side in seconds.

"Jax is nice. I like having him around."

Zack knew she didn't mean that in a romantic sort of way, but that didn't stop the wave of jealousy that swished about because of her saying it.

"He's a good guy."

Ava looked up at him and cocked an eyebrow. "Wait a minute. Are you jealous? You do know I like having you around, too," she said and squeezed his left arm.

Zack ignored the heat puddled on his bicep, even though her touch lasted two seconds. "Why would I be jealous?"

"I don't know. You tell me. Judging by the look in your eyes, I'd say a saw a hint of jealousy for a moment," she said, followed by a chuckle. "Just messing with you. You're big and tough. Not too much bothers you I'd assume."

If she only knew. Everything concerning her bothered him in ways it shouldn't. And apparently that fact was even obvious to his brother Zeke who made it his business to point out the chemistry between him and Ava. For a solid thirty minutes after he returned from seeing Ava back to the apartment safely, Zack listened to Zeke and his assumptions and perceived notions about Ava and Zack. But nothing was going on. He thought he'd done a good job hiding whatever emotions were attempting to surface, however, he couldn't fool Zeke. Had he fooled Ava?

"Nah. Not too much bothers me. You're right."

Thank goodness for Jax returning. "Ready when you guys are."

About forty-five minutes later, they arrived at Houston's George Bush Intercontinental Airport, checked in, cruised through TSA pre-check, and waited in their designated area for first-class boarding. Ava sat next to him while Jax sat directly behind them to watch her back.

"You know I've traveled on behalf of our company before for sales purposes, but never to a manufacturing facility. Don't get me wrong, I've seen our manufacturing operations stateside, but not out of the country. Never thought I'd have to make this sort of trip under these circumstances. Breaks my heart that something like this is happening right under our noses."

Zack resisted the urge to comfort her by covering her hand with his. "The best thing about this situation is that you're on a path to correct it. That's what a good company does—finds and implements solutions. I can respect that."

"Thanks. My mom is distraught, so it must be bad. She's one of the calmest women I know. Easygoing. Not a lot rattles her. But she was upset enough to not want to talk about it when Dad broke the news to me and my sisters."

"Speaking of sisters, why isn't Crystal going on this trip instead of you? Or even Layla?" He would have very much preferred Crystal travel as opposed to Ava, but it was time he stopped fooling himself. A part of him liked the fact that he'd get to spend more time with her.

"Crystal wanted to, but I convinced her that I should go."

"Why'd you do that?"

She looked around, as if checking to make sure no one was listening to their conversation, then she answered, "Because this is important to me, Zack. Crystal needs to focus on running the company and rebuilding her reputation. Layla is head of public relations, so it's her job to help with that. I'm the best person to go, especially since I'm the director of marketing and sales. If I can fix this, I can help us sell more bags and get more distribution deals. The meeting I had the night we met was with Ms. Wertheimer. Partnering with her company would give us the largest distribution deal we've ever had."

An airline attendant announced it was time for first-class passengers to board. Zack and his crew stood and strolled to the attendant, scanned their boarding passes, and made their way through the jetway.

"By the way, I heard what you said back there, and I think it's admirable that you want to do everything you can to help your family's business. And for what it's worth, I think you're the best person to help solve the problem."

Ava turned to him during their walk through the jetway. "Thanks, Zack. That means a lot to me coming from you."

"You're welcome."

When they arrived at their seats, Zack and Ava took the two seats next to each other, while Jax sat directly across from them. Before sitting, Zack scanned the remaining first-class passengers. He was always one to be aware of who sat near him, especially on a twenty-nine-hour trip, although they had two scheduled stops.

Twenty-five minutes later, the plane ascended into the sky, and by the time the captain announced they'd reached cruising altitude, Ava had fallen asleep on his shoulder.

It'd been almost five years since a woman rested on his shoulder, and it felt good. In fact, Ava snuggled against him felt perfect.

Perfect woman. Imperfect circumstances.

∞

Ava's eyelids fluttered open, and her breath caught. There she was all cuddled up with her bodyguard. What must he be thinking of her right now? She hadn't intended to fall asleep on Zack's shoulder. And how long was she asleep? She straightened in her seat. "I'm sorry. It wasn't my intent to use you as my human pillow."

One corner of his lip turned upward. "You don't have to apologize, Ava. I'm not offended in any way." Then he shrugged. "Well, I take that back. That means I'm not as firm as I thought I was if you could sleep so comfortably—and snore at that."

She bugged her eyes. "Why didn't you wake me up if I was snoring?" She looked around the cabin, wondering if anyone heard her.

"Just kidding around with you. You weren't snoring, but you were quite comfortable, so I let you sleep. You obviously needed it."

The flight attendant who seemed to have had a jolt of caffeine or a very good nap like Ava stopped at her seat. "Ma'am, can I get anything for you?"

"Yes, but I need a minute."

"Take your time, and ring me when you're ready," she said before disappearing behind the curtain.

"Thanks." Ava vacated her seat and went into the plane's lavatory to relieve herself and rinse her mouth with mouthwash. Feeling more refreshed, she returned to her seat.

As she neared Zack, a bit of self-consciousness set in. His eyes roamed the length of her in a way she hadn't noticed before. Did he even know he was looking at her with what she could only describe as admiration or appreciation? This couldn't be all in her head, could it? If the circumstances were different, she would have addressed the growing chemistry they seemed to have, but she couldn't—well, wouldn't—say anything for fear of making things uncomfortable between them. And they had a lot more time to spend with each other without her making their interactions awkward.

"Hey. So, what did I miss when I was sound asleep?"

"Clouds, blue skies, and the humming of the plane's engine."

"No action then."

"Just the way we want it to be." The intensity of his eyes was too much for Ava.

To distract herself from the belly flutters Zack's closeness was doing to her, she pulled out her electronic tablet and focused her attention on work—the speech she and Crystal collaborated on to give to their employees. The temporary facilities their team had identified. The incentives they'd provide to their employees in the interim. Whatever it took to keep her mind fixated on anything other than the man's eyes, half-smile, made-for-him woodsy fresh scent, and the way her very being responded to him.

For the duration of the trip, she slept on and off and kept the conversation light when she was awake. Outside of eating with Zack in the airports during their two scheduled stops, she concentrated on work by either scrolling through her tablet or talking on the phone with her sisters.

After twenty-nine hours of travel, Ava could only think about a hot shower and more sleep to adjust to the time difference. She needed time away from Zack in her hotel room to get in the right head space. Once they arrived in Cambodia, went through customs, and traveled another thirty minutes to their hotel, Ava retired to her suite to get cleaned up and rest for a few more hours stretched out in her bed. Though the first-class accommodations were cozier than coach, there was nothing like a nice comfortable bed.

Her suite boasted warm hues of brown, a nice-sized living room, king-sized bed, private study, and elegant dining area. All of which she'd have to spend more time appreciating after she got some sleep.

Before she closed her eyes, she called her father. "Dad, we made it."

"Oh, good. I was about to call and check in on you." His voice was flat. Not exactly the greeting she expected from him. Something had to be wrong, didn't it? She braced her core, waiting for what he'd say next, but no additional words came.

"Okay…Dad, is everything alright?"

"Not really. Something else has happened."

Chapter Twelve

*Z*ack ended the call with his brother Zeke letting him know they'd arrived safely in Cambodia. The next item on his agenda was rest. He didn't sleep as well on the plane because there was nothing like being stretched out on a comfortable mattress, regardless of the accommodations. Everything was in place. Ava settled into her room. Jax claimed his post outside of her door. Unlike him, Jax took full advantage of the extra roomy first-class seat and slept.

He trotted through the suite into the bathroom and turned on the shower. The steam beckoned him inside. Zack removed his shirt, preparing himself for the much-needed time under the stream of hot water.

His phone vibrated on the bathroom counter. Tempted to ignore it, he remembered that he was there on assignment.

Ava.

"Is everything okay?" he asked when he answered the call. Everything within him stiffened, drawing his attention away from the running water.

"I don't think so. I—"

"On my way to your room now."

Zack switched off the shower, slipped his shirt back over his head, grabbed his key card, and galloped out of his room. When he got to her room, which was right next to his, she was already standing in the doorway, the sweet fragrance of her filling his nostrils. Over the past few weeks, he'd grown accustomed to the scent that was purely Ava. Even after the long flight, he still enjoyed the sweet smell of her.

"What happened?" he asked, walking past her into the room, looking around for anything suspicious.

"No, it's nothing in here," she said, placing a soft grip on his bicep, probably an attempt to calm him.

His heart rate slowed, and he turned to her, finally giving her a moment to explain.

"I just talked to my dad. He's on his way up to discuss another message he received—this time in his e-mail."

"Did he say anything else about the e-mail?"

Though he knew there was the likelihood they'd run into issues here, a part of him hoped this would be an uneventful trip.

Ava shook her head. "No, he didn't."

Zack gauged her for a moment. She didn't appear to be bothered by the new message, which was good. He'd been thankful not having to work with someone who lost their composure at every turn.

"You okay? You don't seem concerned by it."

"Should I be worried? I mean, I have you here with me, and I doubt this person is here or even knows we're here, so I'm good. I feel safe with you around."

He could appreciate the sentiments, but he couldn't pretend like the pressure wasn't mounting within him to ensure she didn't suffer the same fate as Mariah. He wouldn't be able to live with himself if something happened to Ava, too, especially under his watch.

"Good. I'm glad you're not shaken by this."

Zack refrained from reaching out to comfort her by rubbing his hands along her arms. He wasn't sure why the urge kept resurfacing. Though he'd been out of the field for a while, he'd never had this issue before Ava. There had to be a way to shake this—her—from his system to prevent her from getting hurt.

Two taps on the door garnered his attention. Zack strolled to the door, checked the visitor's identity through the peep hole, then opened the door to allow Ava's parents, Lamont, and his wife, Dana, inside.

They shuffled in, both wearing identical expressions. Scrunched eyebrows. Creases in their foreheads. Lips turned down.

Lamont shoved the phone into Zack's hand, the screen opened to the e-mail he'd received. Dana went to Ava and wrapped her arms around her neck. Though Ava hadn't appeared upset by the message before now, her features softened more when she was in her mother's embrace.

Zack read the e-mail.

144

Tick tock, Mr. Langston. I'm losing money every day you do nothing. You don't want to see what I have planned next for Ava, do you? One week.

Zack's blood sizzled. He despised cowards. First, if the man had an issue with Lamont, he could have worked to settle it man-to-man. Lamont made himself accessible and didn't seem like the type of person who'd brush off anyone who had concerns about his business practices. Second, he was beginning to take the threats against Ava more personally than he should.

"I can get Zeke to run a trace to find out where the e-mail originated."

Lamont shook his head. "Thanks. I'm getting fed up with this person."

You and me both.

Zack whipped out his own phone and called Zeke. "Hey. Lamont received another message. An e-mail this time. Patch into his phone. Find a location, IP address, to help us track the source."

"Got it. But you do know I know how to do my job, right?"

"Of course. You're the man in charge. Get back with me as soon as you find out anything. No matter the time."

Not that he could personally do anything about the perpetrator thousands of miles away. But still, this situation would likely help them close in on this person much sooner rather than later. A part of Zack was glad the perpetrator made this mistake. It would only be a matter of time before they found them now with the technological tools The Four Kings had developed.

"Got it. I'll even bring in Josh if necessary." Their brother Joshua was the most tech savvy of the four of them and spearheaded many of the tech software programs created by their firm.

"Thanks, bro. Keep me posted."

Zack ended the call and handed Lamont's phone to him. "We're on it. Zeke is running the trace. In the meantime, are you two okay?"

"Yes. We're both at the point where we want this to be over. Hopefully the steps we take over the next few days to begin rectifying the manufacturing situation here will steer us in the right direction."

"Let's hope," Dana said. "Thank you for taking care of our daughter. I know we're paying you, but no amount of money can express our true gratitude."

"You're welcome. Ava makes my job easy." He glanced her way, and one of those smiles that caused his chest to constrict spread across her face.

He caught a glimpse of Lamont who looked between him and Ava and hiked an eyebrow, but he didn't say anything. And Zack was glad about that. It was too late at night to even address such things. He wouldn't have any answers for the man anyway. But Zack had to wonder if the chemistry between him and Ava was evident to Lamont like it had been to Zeke.

She hugged her elbows to her chest, and her smile grew wider in a teasing manner. "I try not to be too hard on you. And speaking of that, I think you could use some rest. So could I." Ava flipped her wrist to check the time. "It's almost two in the morning. Couple that with jetlag and the way our sleep pattern is already messed up, I say we call it a night."

Zack made eye contact with everyone standing in the room. "I can agree with that. Is everyone all good?"

"We're fine now. I trust all will be well. We'll head back to bed and allow you both to get some rest. Is ten reasonable enough for us to go to the manufacturing plant to talk with our employees?" Lamont asked Ava.

"I think I can manage. Zack, is that enough time for you to rest?"

"Yes, it is, and remember that I'm right next door if you need anything at all. But you should be safe. Jax is posted up in the hall."

"Doesn't he need his rest, too?" Dana asked.

"He slept well on the plane at every opportunity, so he's good for now. When Ava and I leave in the morning, he'll rest then as well."

Dana didn't look too convinced, but she didn't say anything else about it. She and Lamont gave their goodnight wishes and returned to their room.

Zack turned to face Ava when he made it to the door.

"What's my number one concern?" he asked.

"My safety."

"Right. So nothing is too small for you to call me. Got it?"

Her eyelids drooped, and she parted her lips, but clamped them shut, obviously rethinking whatever she'd been about to say. "Got it. Good night slash morning. See you in a little while."

∞

Ava was a firm believer in breakfast being the most important meal of the day. But this morning, she happily skipped it to get another hour of sleep. She'd settle for a cup of coffee on her way to the manufacturing facility.

She dressed in a pair of casual pants and a shirt, and slipped into a pair of gym shoes since she'd be walking through the manufacturing facility. Ava packed a pair of ballet flats in her bag to change into after their visit.

Now that she'd had enough rest, she had a few minutes to appreciate the elegant accommodations and the view of Phnom Penh's skyline. Modern furniture. Marble countertops. Crystal light fixtures. She hoped to take advantage of the spa while she was there. A much-needed massage could help her relax despite the circumstances. Not to mention the on-site restaurant she read about on the flight over. Tasty food made everything better, and her mind had been set on dining at the hotel's five star restaurant since seeing photos and reviews online.

Zack rapped on the door with his usual four taps. Ava grabbed her tote and met him at the door. He stood there in his trusty bodyguard snakeskin-wear-everywhere leather jacket with a stone face and piercing serious eyes to match.

"I'm ready. I want to grab a coffee from downstairs before leaving. Mom and Dad are already waiting."

"Sounds good. You look refreshed."

He'd given her a once-over, and she believed she saw a hint of appreciation flash in his eyes. *When are we going to stop playing this game?*

"I am. Had a good night of sleep. Ready to go change the world today. You ready to protect and serve?"

"Always."

Ava double checked to ensure she had her room key before closing the door. Zack turned to Jax. "We're heading out. Time for you to rest, my man."

Jax fist bumped him. "Okay. Call me if you need me."

"You got it."

When they arrived downstairs, her mom and dad were sitting on a cream loveseat in the lobby, huddled close, and involved in an intimate conversation. Her father's back turned to her, but she could see her mother's face. Whatever he was saying to her must have been funny or either endearing because her smile was wide and genuine. She felt Ava staring at them because she glanced up and waved them over.

Lamont stood and turned.

"Good morning. Did the two of you rest well?"

Zack shook Lamont's hand. "I did. Thanks for asking. We'll be ready to go after Ava gets her morning cup of coffee."

Ava left the group, with Zack at her side, and grabbed a cup of the steaming liquid from the coffee bar, doctoring it up with flavored creamer and one packet of sugar substitute. She stirred, blew off the steam, and took a quick sip. "Perfect. Just the way I like it."

When she and Zack rejoined the group, they shuffled toward the exit, with Zack's hand at the small of her back. Like it was the most natural thing to do. Like he did it often. And sure, he intended it to be in a protective sort of way, but her skin sizzled from the contact.

Dressed in all black, their driver rounded the car and opened both the front and back passenger doors. Her dad took the front seat while Ava, her mother, and Zack took the back seat. The driver reminded her of Jeffrey from the nineties' sitcom, *The Fresh Prince of Bel-Air,* right down to his voice.

"Confirming we're returning to the manufacturing district?"

Zack leaned forward. "Yes. Please use the specified route we provided earlier. Thank you, Asher."

Asher opened his phone and looked over a message of what Ava assumed were route instructions before he navigated the car onto the main road. After about fifteen minutes, Ava noticed the area change from well-to-do to not-so-well. In fact, the longer they drove, the area looked worse. From an elegant hotel and nice buildings in the surrounding area to rundown buildings and an area of town that seemed to have been forgotten. As they continued to drive, they entered an area that looked overpopulated with buildings, and long before Asher slowed to a stop, she knew that's where their operations were, and it broke her heart long before she saw the building and the working conditions inside of it.

"You good?" Zack asked, pulling her thoughts away from what she was about to witness.

Ava nodded, but didn't turn her head to look at him, though his eyes were a distraction. And although a distraction would be nice, she needed to focus on work instead of the war in her heart and mind over the man sitting next to her.

She covered her mother's hand with her own. When her mom's eyes met hers, the sadness she'd witnessed the night before was there. Just how bad was it? And would she regret coming to see the workers' situation for herself?

No matter what, you came to help change the situation.

"We're here," Asher announced. He shifted the car into park, got out, and opened the doors for them. Her father had already climbed out of the car and rounded the front of the vehicle to stand next to Asher. "I'll go find a parking space, but I'll be here waiting for you when you're ready to leave." Asher bowed his head and returned to his seat behind the wheel.

Her dad led the way down the dirt path toward the gray one-story building. It was one among four in the area—two of the same sized buildings next to it and one behind it. She wasn't an expert when it came to measurements, so she couldn't estimate square footage, but from the outside, the buildings looked to be a quarter of the size of her local grocery store. And that wasn't saying much.

Ava, her mother, and Zack trailed her dad inside the building. Ava was the first to enter behind her dad. To her left was one small office with two desks, and to her right were rows upon rows of employees. Some of them sat close enough that they reminded her of a bunch of bananas. How could they even efficiently do their jobs?

A short man with straight, thinning black hair greeted them. He bowed first, then said, "Good morning. We've been expecting you, Mr. Langston." He then turned to the rest of them and introduced himself. "I'm Ray, the supervisor. I understand you have concerns. Is that right?"

Ava could hardly make out the conversation between her father and Ray. The chiming and clinking of the machinery drowned them out. Ray invited them into his office, but with the desks and chairs inside, there wasn't much room for the five of them, so Ava, her mother, and Zack declined.

She watched the two of them through the glass window though and assumed her father shared their plan to move them into a better facility, pay while the transition happened, and an increase in salaries over time. And Ava only assumed as much because the man's eyes grew wide, and a smile stretched across his face. Ray grabbed her father's hand and bounced it up and down. Yep, that had to have been what he shared.

Her father whipped out his phone and made a call—to Crystal, she assumed. Ray must have loved everything she said to him because his smile didn't fade. After the call ended, her dad tucked his phone back into his pocket and followed Ray back out to the area where they left the trio standing. Ray pressed a button on the wall, and a buzzer sounded. The machines ceased, employees stilled, and all eyes were locked in on the group.

Ray introduced her dad, who in turn introduced her and her mother. He whispered to Ava, "Go on. Give them the good news."

Ava parted her lips, but the words wouldn't come at first. She had to choke back the emotion that welled within her.

Emotion from the fact that it was their company that had them in this position to begin with.

And emotion because they were also changing that.

She took a deep breath to steady her nerves. She wasn't one to have an issue with public speaking, but this moment was tough.

"Good morning."

Murmurs of good morning came from the employees before her.

Ava locked eyes with several of them before continuing, hoping they'd sense her sincerity. "We apologize for having you work under these conditions. This is not what Langston Brands is about. We care about our employees, and as of today, each of you can go home with pay until we can improve your working conditions by moving you to a better facility with adequate space and air conditioning."

A few shouts rang out, but most employees wore blank expressions. Ray stepped forward to translate. After he finished, the entire room erupted in applause, high fives, and others with hands raised to God in praise.

The expressions of joy. The smiles. This moment made the trip worth it.

They were on the path of getting their company back on track.

Chapter Thirteen

Crystal had given Ava and their father permission to meet with the commercial real estate agent she'd located in Phnom Penh to view three potential properties to move their manufacturing operations. Ava hadn't expected that task to take all day. They met downstairs at eleven that morning, and now it was seven in the evening. Where had the time gone? The Realtor suggested they save the last property for the next day, but Ava wanted this process to move as quickly as possible. No need putting off for tomorrow what she could do today. And now her stomach regretted it and regretted skipping breakfast.

When Asher pulled the car in front of the hotel entrance and opened their doors, Ava scurried inside with Zack, of course, at her side.

"I'm going to get cleaned up for dinner. Twenty minutes tops," she said to him when they stepped on the elevator. Her parents were staying on the first floor.

"Take as much time as you need. I'll be waiting in my room."

"Are you kidding me? If it takes me any longer, you have my permission to burst through my door to make sure I haven't passed out. I'm so hungry I could eat you right now."

That one-sided smirk touched a corner of his lips. Ava burst into laughter.

She recovered, and for the first time noticed the mellow music coming from the elevator speakers. "That didn't come out right, but you get my point. I'm starving, but I want to get cleaned up first."

"I'm literally at your service and ready whenever you are."

Ava plucked the collar of his leather jacket. "Let me guess: You'll be wearing this?"

Zack glanced down at his jacket then back up at Ava. He scrunched his brows. "What's wrong with my jacket?"

The elevator dinged, and Ava stepped off. "Oh, nothing. It gives you this handsome, mysterious look. Suits you, and I like it."

Did I really just say that out loud?

"Thanks. It's my favorite."

She did the opposite of what she should have done. Ava looked into his eyes. Pulled into those hypnotic contraptions, she almost did yet another thing she shouldn't have done. But before that could happen, they arrived at her suite, and she disappeared behind the door as fast as she could.

Breathe.

Ava almost despised the fact that she was so attracted to him. On one hand, she enjoyed the feeling because it was unlike anything

156

she'd ever experienced in her life. And on the other, nothing could quite come of this thing between them with him being her bodyguard and all.

I've got to get over this thing.

After a five-minute shower and rushing through her cosmetic and dressing routine, she was ready with one minute to spare. She texted Zack, *Ready.*

Thirty seconds later, Zack knocked on her door, and her growling stomach answered.

"New perfume?"

Surprised he'd noticed, she said, "Yes, it is. A gift from Layla." But she shouldn't be too surprised. Zack noticed everything.

When they arrived downstairs, she received a text from her mom.

We're tired and plan to just take dinner in our room. You have reservations at Brasserie Louis. You and Zack enjoy.

So much for getting over this thing her emotions conjured up regarding him. Ava and Zack sauntered up to the hostess station where Ava gave them her name for the reservation.

"Looks like my parents won't be joining us. What about Jax?"

"No. He already ate and wants to rest up before he's back on duty once you're in your room for the evening."

Then it was settled. It would be just the two of them. Alone. And the comfortable seating for two in front of the large windowpanes facing the skyline made it feel like a date. But their

157

time together this evening was far from romantic. In fact, romance should be the furthest thing from her brain right now when her thoughts were clouded with how long it would take for her family to move their business forward.

Zack took the seat in front of the window. He didn't like sitting with his back toward everyone. Too much risk, and it put him at a disadvantage to act quickly if something happened. So Ava sat across from him getting the skyline view, which was fine by her.

Perusing the menu, Ava asked, "What looks good to you? I'm going for the *Soupe de Chou et Légumes Mirepoix, Consommé de Volaille* as an appetizer."

"You don't have to show off in front of me. Using the English terms is fine."

Ava chuckled. "Vegetable and cabbage soup in chicken broth."

"No appetizer for me. I'll just go with the Australian ribeye."

Their waitress appeared tableside with glasses of water and to take their orders. When she left, Ava turned her attention back to Zack.

"I want to ask you something, and I don't want you to take any offense to it. I'm totally okay if you choose not to answer."

Zack braced his elbows on the table and clasped his hands. "Go for it."

"When we met, you mentioned that you were out protecting someone else when you should have been protecting your wife. What happened to her?"

A darkness clouded Zack's eyes, and Ava regretted asking. She leaned back in her chair. "Sorry if I'm overstepping."

"No, I don't mind sharing," he said, but based on the tightness in his jaw, she got the feeling he didn't want to talk about it. He maintained his position on the table, but broke eye contact and looked past her as if he could see the memory.

"As usual, I was working a case. This one was a political client. One night, I was with him at a debate when I received an alert that my house alarm had been activated. I called to reach Mariah, and when she didn't answer, I should have left to go check on her. I didn't immediately worry because she often forgot to turn the alarm off before going into the house. I tried her a few more times, and then that's when Zeke called. He was close to my house and went to go make sure everything was okay, but it wasn't. He found my house broken into and Mariah on the living room floor with three gunshot wounds in her chest. They took her wedding ring, purse, and jewelry box."

"And you blame yourself," Ava said softly.

"I should have been there, Ava. I should've been there. As her husband, it was my job to protect her, and I didn't."

Ava's heart shattered into tiny pieces. Reacting purely from instinct, she unlaced his fingers, placed both of her palms into his, and squeezed his hands.

"I'm sorry this happened to her—and to you. If you've been carrying this guilt around with you since her death, you have to release it, Zack. It's not your fault because you didn't fire the gun.

And yes, things may have turned out differently if you were there, but you have to find solace in the love you two shared. Hold on to that. I didn't know her, but I believe she wouldn't have wanted you to blame yourself."

"Thanks, Ava," he said, returning the squeeze.

"And since we're asking personal questions, it's my turn."

"Okay. That's fair."

But what wasn't fair was that he still held her hands.

What wasn't fair was that his eyes had once again engaged hers in a lost battle.

What wasn't fair was that she was at a disadvantage because of what his touch did to her.

"Tell me why you aren't married or at least in a serious relationship."

Ava hesitated before answering. Her logic made sense to her, but sharing it out loud brought about a vulnerability she wasn't sure she should expose herself to. But then again, she trusted Zack with her life. Trusting him with her heart wasn't a requirement in this arrangement.

She released a heavy sigh. "I just haven't met the right man to marry. It might sound fairytale or romance novelish, but aside from him being a man of faith with a strong work ethic, when I see him or even hear his voice, I want to experience flutters in my belly, kisses that make my toes curl, and just plain ol' genuine, pure passion and connection. When he looks at me, I want to feel like no other woman in this world matters. And I understand that's a huge ask from men these days, but I won't settle for anything less." She shrugged. "If it even exists."

What she couldn't say was that he gave her those flutters, and every time he looked at her, her soul stirred. Like now. She could get lost in the depths of his eyes—eyes that held such compassion and warmth.

Still holding her hands snug in his, Zack ran his thumbs across the back of her hand. "You deserve everything your heart desires. I'm pretty sure that one day you'll get what you want. Just be patient."

Patient with you?

"Here is your appetizer, *Soupe de Chou et Légumes Mirepoix, Consommé de Volaille,*" their waitress announced.

Ava broke their connection so the waitress could place the bowl of soup on the table. With her hands no longer in his, an emptiness washed over her.

This is crazy.

"Be careful. It's hot," the waitress said, sliding the bowl on the table. "You two celebrating an anniversary?" The woman beamed.

"Oh, no," both she and Zack said in unison.

"We're just..." Ava looked from the waitress and back to Zack. "Friends."

"Oh." Confusion clouded her face, then she hiked an eyebrow as if to ask, *Are you sure?* She smiled and added, "Sometimes we're the last to know."

What was that supposed to mean?

Ava bowed her head to bless her food and to also ask God to help her regain control over her emotions, which were spiraling every second she spent with this man. Before she could start her prayer, she felt Zack's hand cover one of hers, and he blessed their food. When he finished, she had to ask God for forgiveness. She couldn't concentrate on the prayer because of the way Zack lit the entire right side of her body on fire from his touch.

"Amen, and thank you," Ava said.

Were they having a moment? They were definitely having a moment.

Ava tasted her soup to distract herself and to come up with something less personal to talk about.

"So what do you do when you're not looking out for others? How do you look out for you?"

"Sports—basketball, football, baseball, soccer, anything really."

"So do you cheer for the home teams?"

"No doubt. It would help if they won a few games, but I'm still down for the cause."

"The Astros seem to be the only home team making us proud these days." Ava took another spoonful of soup into her mouth.

"You're a sports fan?"

Ava chuckled. "Not in the slightest. I just catch the scores on the nightly news."

"Live sporting events are more entertaining than watching on TV. We should go sometime. Maybe I can change your fan status."

Did he just ask me out?

Her spoon was raised halfway to her lips. She paused and waited for him to catch or correct himself, but he never did. But he'd realized what he'd done because he stopped to sip his water. Relief washed over his face when the waitress returned with their entrees. They spent the rest of dinner talking about random things like TV sitcoms and movies—well, Ava did most of the talking, ending the evening with her committing to make him sit through a romantic movie.

When they made it back upstairs to her room, Zack took a quick scan of her suite to ensure all was well before bidding her goodnight.

"Wait," she'd said when he reached the door.

Ava crossed the room and stood in front of him. She needed to know if she was imagining the chemistry between them. And given she'd never made the first move with a man in her life, she squeezed her hands to still the trembles. Against her better judgment, and risking rejection and future awkwardness between them, Ava said, "Aside from the whole work dynamic, you being my bodyguard and me being your client, am I crazy to think that something is happening between us? There's this pull that I—"

Zack drew her into his arms and solidified what her heart already knew. When his lips connected with hers, her knees buckled.

Thankfully, his hold was firm enough to keep her from falling. That same connection she felt whenever they touched was ever present and much stronger. He massaged the back of her head as he expertly caressed her lips with his own, branding her heart with his name.

"Good night, Ava."

And without another word, he disappeared on the other side of the door, leaving her toes curled and heart in the red zone.

With one kiss, he'd ruined her.

∞

Zack regretted nothing.

And that's what shook him. He'd been fighting his growing feelings for Ava using his job as her protector and his dead wife as a shield. But whatever this pull was between them blasted through that armor and momentarily took hold of him.

But it couldn't happen again.

No matter how perfect she felt in his arms.

No matter the connection they shared.

No matter how right they seemed to be for each other.

Back inside his suite, Zack plopped down into the chair in the sitting room. Massaging his chin, he thought back to what he'd done—he'd crossed the line.

His actions were simply unprofessional. They weren't on this trip to fall in love or pursue romantic interests. This was business. All of it. His mind knew it. He just wished he didn't have to fight so hard for his heart and emotions to understand it.

And he should apologize to Ava because he wouldn't do anything to jeopardize her safety. Yet, an apology would be insincere since he enjoyed every single second. And Ava did too. She melted in his arms, which encouraged him to pour all of himself into that kiss.

When he couldn't stew in his thoughts any longer, Zack showered and went to bed. Thoughts and dreams of Ava held him captive. Sleep evaded him, so he climbed out of bed and did the one thing that cleared his mind—or at least gave him something to focus on other than whatever bothered him: work.

With Philip Harper being a question mark, he moved to the next person on his list. Zack reviewed the financials, criminal history, social media content, known associates, and every other document he had on Rachel Williams. No criminal history—or at least she'd never been caught because her fingerprints weren't in the criminal database. No money problems that he could see. With the millions of dollars she had, she wouldn't care enough about her investment in Langston Brands to hurt anyone. Unconvinced she had any hand in the threats against Ava, he moved to the third person on his list, Brian Bissell. And after spending another hour perusing documents concerning him, Zack came to the same conclusion as he had with Rachel.

He had to be missing something or even looking in the wrong direction.

Zack flipped his wrist and checked the time, 3:00 a.m. That meant it was roughly 2:00 p.m. back in Houston. He phoned Zeke.

"Hey. Everything okay out there?"

"Yeah. It's fine. No issues. But I want to run something by you. Tell me what you think."

"Okay. Shoot."

"I've gone through the files of the top three shareholders. I've seen nothing that would make me think any of them would harm Ava based on their financial statuses—criminal history either. Maybe I'm missing something. You've seen the files, right? What do you think?"

"I'm inclined to agree with you," Zeke said. "I read your notes about the Philip guy, and although he isn't quite off your list, you still think you're looking in the wrong direction?"

"Yeah, I do. A smart criminal wouldn't lead us right to them. Insinuating in their notes that they're a shareholder is too easy. Whoever this person is would need personal access to both Lamont and Ava. Who would've known she was out to dinner that night or that she wouldn't be home to leave the note? And the e-mail was sent to Lamont's personal e-mail address, which isn't public knowledge," Zack said more to himself than to Zeke.

"Okay. Sounds to me like you already have a name."

Zack shared his suspicions with Zeke before ending the call. Zeke would use their internal software to run reports and send them to Zack as soon as possible. A mixed level of comfort and uneasiness settled within him.

What if the person he was looking for had been in front of his face this entire time?

166

Chapter Fourteen

Ava lay in bed held hostage by thoughts of the kiss. It was all she thought about last night, and it continued to consume her that morning. When she asked if there was something between them, that wasn't the response she had in mind. However, she wasn't complaining. No one had ever kissed her that way—with such passion. And she no longer wondered if kisses could make her toes curl because Zack proved that to be true. Talk about toe curling, soul stirring, heart racing, and pearl clutching. Zack's lips on hers did all of that and more.

It was simply unreal. So unreal that she felt like she needed him to kiss her again just so she could be certain she didn't imagine the feelings.

Though her thoughts craved to stay in bed and think about all things Zack, she couldn't. She had work to do. In two hours, she and her parents would meet with Crystal and Layla via video conference. Eight in the morning was the happy medium. That way, it was seven in the evening for Crystal and Layla, which meant that their normal duties should be taken care of. Crystal tended to work late most days, so late meetings didn't bother her unless she and Marcel had a date.

Once showered and dressed, Ava downed her first cup of morning coffee. She fought against the idea to text Zack. What would she say anyway? Why did this thing have to be complicated?

Until her parents arrived, she checked e-mail, scanned social media, and perused her streaming service's latest movie offerings.

Three determined taps on the door alerted her to Jax—she'd distinguished his and Zack's knocking rhythm. Ava opened the door.

"Hey, Mom and Dad. Come on in. Jax, do you need anything? Water? Coffee? Bathroom? You can take a break since my parents are in here with me."

"All good. Thanks, Miss Langston."

Ava knew Zack relieved Jax from time to time, but she always made a point to ask him if he could use the rest. It had to be tiring and lonely standing outside of her door.

Back inside, the look on her dad's face gave her pause. She hated when he wore that concerned frown. What else could go wrong at this point? Weren't they on a good path?

"Give it to me straight," Ava said as she sat across from the two of them. Her mom sat close to her dad, their knees touching, a supportive hand on his back. That was the *we're about to have a serious conversation* pose.

Ava grabbed a decorative pillow and pulled it to her chest.

"One of the reasons we skipped dinner last night is because I had another conversation with Ray. There were about fifty underage employees that he released yesterday. As a measure of compliance, we'll set up procedures to ensure this doesn't happen again. What's most concerning is that we've learned someone in our corporate office authorized underage workers, along with the poor working conditions to save money."

Ava sucked in a breath. Her heart pounded. Couldn't be either of her sisters, could it? "Who was it?"

Her father's lips pulled into a straight line, and he shook his head. Whoever it was had to be someone he trusted. The disappointed look on his face crushed her heart. Ava joined him and her mom on the small sofa and put a supporting hand on the other side of his back.

Her mom answered instead. "It was Rick."

"You've got to be kidding me." Frozen in her seat, Ava thought about Rick's behavior. He wanted to be CEO. Though she didn't like him, he'd always proven himself loyal to Langston Brands. The way he acted about her and her meeting with Wertheimer, why would he do this? Was he also the one behind the threats on her life?

Ava shook her head. "I can't believe this."

"Neither can I. Rick has been with us for years, and I've trusted him. It pains me to think he would hurt our company this way, causing us so much damage and costing us so much money. It isn't as much about the money but about the idea that he betrayed my trust and confidence."

"I'm so sorry, Dad. Do Crystal and Lay know?"

"Not yet. We'll discuss it on the call today. I'm not in charge anymore—Crystal is—but I will highly recommend his immediate termination."

"I doubt you have to worry about Crystal firing him, Dad. Crystal won't stand for this. She and the rest of us love the company too much to let this slide."

He released a half-hearted snort. "I'm sure of it."

Ava took a deep breath and asked the question burning in the back of her mind. "Do you think Rick is behind the threats?"

"I don't know anything anymore; however, I don't think Rick would hurt you or even threaten to do so. He wouldn't want to have to deal with me. I'm sure he thought he'd be able to keep the sweatshop running without it being traced back to him."

"Rick isn't crazy enough to threaten your life," her mom added.

Though neither of them had the facts, she felt a little relief. Ava's eyes snapped up. "Why didn't you come down to dinner to tell me about it—or at least call or text?"

Her parents shared a look before her mom said, "Actually, we did come to the restaurant, but you and your bodyguard seemed to be having a...moment, so your dad and I decided this piece of information could wait until morning."

If her skin was light enough, it would have turned red. Shoot, for all she knew, it probably was red. Ava had nothing else to add nor did she want to explain something she didn't quite understand.

And thankfully they didn't ask questions. She flipped her wrist to check her watch.

Ava stood. "It's about time to sign in for the meeting. I'll grab my laptop."

Ava set up the laptop and logged into the video portal. Crystal and Layla were already there. It was good to see their faces. Ava smiled.

"Good morning, good evening. How are you two doing?"

"We're good, considering the circumstances. What about you? Is Zack still keeping you safe?" Layla asked.

Ava smiled and nodded. "All good here."

"*Hmmm.* Looks that way. We'll talk about it when the meeting is over," Crystal said.

Crystal opened the meeting, inviting their father to say a prayer before they began.

"Father God, thank You for Your goodness and mercy. Thank You for Your power at work in our lives. Your favor even when we don't deserve it, and Your forgiveness that You freely give. Guide us as we navigate tough decisions and help lead us on the best path forward for our family and the business that You've blessed us to have. In Jesus' name. Amen."

"Amen," the rest of the group said in chorus.

"Thanks, Dad. And again, thank you, Mom, Dad, and Ava for standing in my place out in Phnom Penh. Now for the update on the properties you all viewed yesterday."

"Based on our needs, I believe property number three is the most viable option. It's a lower monthly payment than the other two properties, provides more space, better ventilation, and is overall more suitable for production. You should have videos of all three properties in your e-mail.

"I looked them over, and Lay and I agree that property three is the best option. I discussed it with Rick this morning, and he is concerned about profit. I had Shantina, our finance manager, run a profit analysis. We may be in the red for at least six months, unless we can secure the deal with Wertheimer. In that case, we could cut that time in half. I'm okay with that. I think we can all agree that how we treat our employees is just as important as our bottom line. They are our biggest asset, and we have to treat them as such."

Lamont wore a proud father smile and nodded his agreement.

"I'll get the Realtor on the phone after our meeting and see what it'll take to expedite this process. He informed me that it wouldn't be a problem securing a contract on either property."

Relief settled in Crystal's features as she relaxed in her seat. Her shoulders were now less rigid. "Thanks, Dad. We can get Rick to oversee this project from here so you guys can come home."

"Rick is the reason we're in this mess," their mother, Dana, piped in. Up until this point, she'd been relatively quiet.

"What do you mean, Mom?" Layla asked.

Dana deferred to Lamont, who shared the details of Rick's betrayal. Both Crystal and Layla's eyes bugged. Ava imagined she wore the same look when she first found out.

"He is so fired," Crystal seethed. "How dare he challenge me for my seat as CEO when he's working to cut corners, putting our business at risk? I ought to snap his neck."

"Please don't go back to jail," Layla joked.

Ava snickered, the only other person finding the joke funny.

"I don't need to remind you to keep it professional, do I?" Lamont asked.

"No, sir. I can handle Rick."

Ava eyed her big sister. Though she was upset, Ava caught the glimmer in her eyes. No doubt she'd looked forward to the moment she could fire Rick.

"Good."

Layla snapped her fingers as if she'd just remembered something important. "Oh, Ava, does Zack know? Does he think Rick might have something to do with your poisoning or those threats you received?"

"I haven't talked to Zack about any of this yet. I just found out. When we're done with our call, I'll reach out to him and give him an update. If he has any suspicions about Rick after this, I will let y'all know."

"Okay then. Anything else we need to discuss?"

"Crystal and Marcel are going out for a late dinner, so she's trying to rush off the call," Layla said.

Crystal waved her off. "Ignore her. I have plenty of time."

"That's it for me." Their father stood with their mother following suit. "I'm going to call our realtor to get things moving on securing this new property."

"Sounds good. Thanks, Dad," Crystal said.

Ava stood to hug them both. "See you two later."

Once their parents left Ava's room, Layla said, "Okay, give us the deets before you go. What's up with that smile you had when I asked you about Zack earlier? Honey, you are beaming."

"Nothing has changed. He's still doing his job," Ava lied.

Everything changed last night when he'd kissed her. How was she even supposed to face him today?

"See. I don't even know why you're playing," Layla said, laughing.

If Ava didn't know any better, she'd think Layla was privy to the kiss she and Zack had shared. But Layla was her sister and was doing what she normally did—fish for information. Ava would not take the bait.

"I don't normally agree with Layla too quickly regarding relationship stuff, but she's right, li'l sis. You are glowing. It's enough for me to just admit you like him. I don't need any details, unlike Li'l Miss Nosey."

Hours ago, when she'd admitted she liked him, she'd gotten kissed senseless. But these were her sisters. If nothing else, they were secret keepers.

Ava released a heavy breath. "I'm only going to say this once. Lay, there are no details, and nothing has happened. I do like him though—a lot." Ava threw herself back against the sofa and stared at the ceiling, feeling like a high school girl at a slumber party divulging information about her secret crush. "And I don't even know how or why this happened. And what's even crazier is that we can't do anything about it because of the dynamics of our relationship—him being the bodyguard and me being his client. It just doesn't look right."

When she was met with silence, she sat up to check the computer screen. Had she lost connection? Nope. Crystal and Layla both stared at the screen, nearly identical, with their mouths hanging open.

Ava frowned. "What?"

Layla was the first to speak. "Okay, so I was just kidding around a little, but not only do you like him, you're like head over heels. Wow."

Crystal's thoughts were churning. Ava could tell by the way she cocked her head to the side and creased her eyebrows. "Wait a minute. Back up. You said, 'We can't do anything about it.' Does this mean he knows how you feel, he feels the same way, and you two have agreed that you won't pursue a relationship because he's your bodyguard?"

"That's not what I'm saying, and talking about this has just made me realize that I don't want to talk about it right now—just too complicated."

Layla leaned away from the screen with her arms folded across her chest. "Just wow."

Ava's phone vibrated. A message from Zack popped up on the screen.

Z: Are you awake?

Ava's trembling thumb hovered over her phone's keyboard.

A: Yes.

"I need to go."

"Before you do, I just want to say that it really isn't as complicated as you make it seem. Even though you all met under unusual circumstances, nothing can stop two grown people who are determined to be together. Talk to you later." Crystal winked and ended the video call.

If only it were that easy.

∞

Zack met Jax outside of Ava's door, giving him the okay to rest for a while since he'd be with Ava for a few hours. When Jax disappeared, Zack rapped on Ava's door. He'd spent the morning convincing himself that nothing had changed between them and they could continue as before, but when she opened the door dressed like an angel in a long royal blue dress that swept the floor, his heart skipped a few beats. He was sure of it. He slapped his chest a couple of times to restart the rhythm.

"Hey. You okay? Need some water?"

She rushed inside to the mini fridge.

Zack followed her inside but didn't move from the door. He stood in the spot—the spot where the kiss happened. All the thoughts he attempted to store in the back of his mind broke free. And all he could think about was kissing her again.

Ava handed him a bottled water and retreated to the couch in the sitting area, hugging a pillow to her chest. "I have a bit of news to share with you."

Zack snapped out of his own thoughts, accepted the water, and followed her to the couch. Good. She wanted to talk about business. Business was good. Business was why they were here in the first place. Why did he suddenly need to cement those thoughts in his mind?

His eyes perked up when Ava shared about Rick's hand in the sweatshop ordeal. Maybe looking into Rick wasn't the wrong direction after all.

"I talked to Zeke this morning after going through my files on the second and third shareholders. Something tells me I'm looking in the wrong direction, and I said as much to Zeke. In full transparency, I've got my eyes on Rick and Ms. Wertheimer, and given what you've just shared about Rick, that makes me even more suspicious of him."

Ava looked doubtful. "*Ehhh,* I don't know if he has it in him, but I guess we can't be too sure about it since he's the one who started the sweatshop."

"Right. Everyone is fair game while we're completing our investigation."

"Oh, I understand that. Do what you need to do. But why Ms. Wertheimer?"

"She was the only person at the table with you. Full access. How do we know she didn't slip something into your food or drink?"

"I was there the entire time. She doesn't seem like the type either, but I know nothing anymore."

"I'll let you know what I find out. In the meantime, please don't take any more meetings with her."

"That might be tough. She is actually one of the first people I need to meet with when I get back to the States. I need to secure this deal for our company, especially since we're having to make costly changes due to Rick's poor decisions."

Zack leaned forward with his elbows on his knees. She'd obviously perceived that he softened up on her. Images of Mariah's dead body came to mind. That wouldn't happen to Ava. "While I understand your need to do what's best for your company, understand my need to protect you. No meetings with Wertheimer until I've cleared her. Do we have an understanding, Ava?"

His voice held a sternness that was a bit too much, even for his own ears. But Ava needed to be reminded that her safety was most important to him. Not her feelings. He could deal with her being upset and alive, but what he couldn't stomach was her death because he jeopardized her safety by prioritizing her happiness.

"Oh, I understand everything. Completely."

Chapter Fifteen

Zack couldn't have made it any clearer that their involvement was a business arrangement. How dare she think for just a second that they could somehow find their way to each other on the other side of this? That kiss meant nothing to him obviously. It was an impulse. An action he took on a whim. He hadn't even acknowledged it when he came to her room that morning. And although she knew better than to let her guard down, she'd somehow lost control, and now her feelings were hurt.

Ava almost wanted to cancel her touring plans since Zack had to be there, too. From here until the end of his assignment, she wanted to limit her contact with him, but that meant staying inside. Secluded. Hiding. In the name of safety. All she'd be doing is punishing herself.

Ava squared her shoulders and put on her best poker face before meeting Zack in the hallway. She wouldn't let him see that his actions bothered her. He didn't owe her anything and vice versa.

"Hey, Jax. Can I get you anything?"

"I'm all good, Miss Ava. I appreciate you asking."

"You're welcome." She turned to Zack. "I'm ready when you are."

He stepped back a foot and squinted at her. He could sense that her behavior was different, which was fine by her, but he didn't mention it. If she had to guess, it was probably because Jax stood with them.

"Let's head out. Jax, I'll call when we're headed back to the hotel."

"Sounds good."

"You sure you don't want to come see the Royal Palace?" Ava piped in, "It's not every day you get to see a palace. You should come." *And keep me from being alone with this man.*

"Castles aren't really my thing, and boss man here has you covered. A nap sounds like a better idea to me."

"You're missing out," Ava sang.

Jax chuckled, something she'd never seen from him before now. "I'll take my chances. Have fun."

Ava and Zack headed toward the elevator in silence. Once they stepped inside, he looked as if he wanted to talk about something, but reservations kept him silent, she assumed. Completely fine by her.

An hour later, they strolled along the stone path where children fed and chased birds. For an inkling of a second, Ava envisioned herself with her own children but shook the thought from her mind. She wasn't even in a serious relationship with marriage on the horizon.

Palm trees lined one side of the path, and oak trees lined the other. Ava and Zack paid their ten-dollar entry fee and strolled onto the grounds of the Royal Palace in Phnom Penh where a group sat near the entrance playing what looked like xylophones and drums. Every structure in sight was gold or trimmed in gold. Several people lined up outside a smaller temple near the front entrance, holding several white tulips.

"Only once in a king's life does he sit on the throne, and that's when he's coronated," she heard a guide say. That was something she hadn't heard before, so Ava wasn't certain if it was true. It was certainly contradictory to what she'd seen on TV.

"Did you hear what he said?" she asked Zack.

"The tour guide who just walked past us?"

Ava repeated the statement to Zack.

"It's an interesting fact. Haven't heard that before, not that I keep up with the lives of royalty."

"Same."

They walked past the door leading to the king's chambers, which were in the throne hall, the main building of the Royal Palace. They couldn't go inside or take pictures, so they had to admire it from the outside.

Groundkeepers were onsite manicuring trees into spiral shapes she didn't recognize.

Within the palace complex, there was another famous landmark, the Silver Pagoda, a Buddhist temple. They strolled inside in silence, admiring the silver floor tiles, which they learned weighed more than five tons. They couldn't take pictures inside of the Silver Pagoda either.

They strolled by a gated gray stupa with the remains of the twentieth century Cambodian king, Norodum Sihanouk, and a white stupa dedicated to King Ang Duong. After touring the grounds, noting several other neat buildings with the gold Cambodian-style rooftops, they called it a day.

∞

Zack spent the better part of the day in disbelief.

Were they having a fight?

And how could that even be possible when they weren't dating? Why did this woman have him questioning if he'd done anything wrong and how he could or should make it up to her? Insane. All of it. And he had no idea how to even deal with such a situation. Given the dynamics of their relationship, how could he professionally address this attitude she had with him? Anytime she said anything to him, it was short. If he asked her anything, her responses were clipped. Not her usual self.

He'd bet the shoes on his feet that her behavior was intentional.

She'd proven something was bothering her when she cancelled the sunset cruise—an activity she seemed adamant about doing on the plane ride over to Phnom Penh. After their trip to the Royal Palace, she claimed that her head was pounding and she needed rest. A lot of gibberish about her not sleeping well last night.

Couple that with work that needed to be done, and that was the end of the day for her with room service for dinner.

Zack sat in his room thinking back over the chain of events since last night. He half-heartedly scrolled through his own laptop while he thought about what could possibly be wrong with Ava. Was she offended by the kiss? He cancelled that idea. Though he'd crossed the line, Ava wasn't the least bit offended when her body softened in his arms. He'd known her long enough to know she would have slapped him, and he never would have entertained the thought if he thought she'd have any reservations.

Under different circumstances, this would be a moment when he'd seek Zeke's bad advice and do the opposite. But he couldn't tell Zeke what he'd done—thrown professionalism to the wind and given in to matters of the heart. Zeke wouldn't believe the story anyway.

He and Ava needed to talk, but where would they begin?

He texted her.

Z: Are you available to talk for a few minutes?

A: Is this about the case?

Zack huffed and shook his head. While he shouldn't let it bother him that she'd assume any communication from him would be about the case, he was deeply offended. Professional Zack should say no and put his phone away, but Zack the man whose ego was slightly bruised needed to talk this out and make it right if he could. This new strain she'd created didn't sit well with him.

Z: No, it isn't. Can we talk?

Zack watched the conversation bubbles appear on the screen, disappear, then reappear again. She shouldn't be getting under his skin in this way. And he was partially mad at himself for allowing things to go this far. But they were here now, and they had to deal with this situation like adults.

A: Ok. Come over in fifteen minutes.

Chapter Sixteen

Ava paced the floor and wrung her fingers. She had to calm down before Zack came over to talk. If this pending discussion wasn't about work, then it had to be about the kiss. Right?

Crystal's words rang in her mind. *Nothing can stop two grown people who are determined to be together.* But Ava doubted that was the case with Zack. It was hard to read the man. One minute he was kissing her, and the next he was back to being her bodyguard, telling her what she could and couldn't do. Nothing could work between them even if they wanted it to—at least not right now.

Zack's familiar taps sounded on the door. With one long inhale and exhale, she strolled across the suite to let him in.

"Hey," she said and opened the door wider so he could come inside.

"Hey."

Even speaking to each other was awkward.

Ava sat on the small sofa, leaving space for Zack to claim the spot next to her. A love seat was what she'd grown accustomed to calling it, but how ironic was that? There was no love between the two of them.

"So, you wanted to talk? I'm listening." She tucked a foot under her bottom and pulled a pillow to her chest.

Zack sat next to her, shifting to face her. Several seconds passed before he said anything. They sat there looking into each other's eyes. The warmth and understanding she saw there chipped away at her resolve. She was determined to be upset and put space between them, but when she looked at him, all she wanted to do was snuggle into his protective arms. Ava was the first to look away, reaching for a bottle of water and taking the slowest sip she could manage.

He must have been waiting until he had her full attention because he didn't speak until she put the water bottle back on the table.

"I don't know what's happening or why it feels like we're having some sort of fight. Are we? Have I done something to upset you?"

"What makes you think I may be upset with you?"

"You were different today. Your energy was off." He shrugged. "You hardly said anything at all during the palace tour, plus you canceled the sunset cruise. And I distinctly remember you saying that if you didn't do anything else, you wanted to take that cruise and watch the sunset. And I don't buy the fact that you weren't feeling well. So be straight with me. Is this about the kiss?

I won't apologize for kissing you because I did exactly what I wanted to do, and I got the vibe you wanted it and enjoyed it, too."

Oh, I wanted it, and I could kick myself because I want more.

"But if that's what this is about, I won't do it again. My first mission is to protect you, and I'm serious about that."

"See? That's just it." Ava leaped out of her seat and paced in front of him, ticking her points off on her fingertips. "One minute, we're having a moment, connecting, and you lay a kiss on me that made my knees weak. Then the next minute, you're flipping back into G.I. Joe mode telling me what I can and can't do and who I should and shouldn't meet with. Trust me, I understand you have a job to do, but I just can't reconcile between the man I'm starting to care about and the one who's here to protect me."

Zack stood and pulled her into his arms.

There he was confusing her again.

"This is my fault, and I apologize. I allowed my emotions to drive me, and I shouldn't have. It won't happen again, Ava."

With her face still buried in his chest, she asked, "So what does this mean?"

"It is not my intent to cause any confusion. So this means that from now on, I'll focus on my duty to protect you."

They weren't a couple, yet this felt like a breakup. Ava nodded. It had to be this way between them, but she didn't have to like it. They could revisit this situation whenever he caught the person behind the threats. That should give her enough time to reassess her feelings about him and ensure she didn't have some sort of hero complex because he'd saved her and continued to protect her. That sort of thing could mess with a woman's mind, though she was ninety-nine percent sure that wasn't the case here.

Ava collected one last squeeze before breaking their embrace. "I understand."

"Get some rest, and I'll see you in the morning."

Zack left her suite, but it also felt like he'd taken her heart with him.

∞

Establishing boundaries should have been a good thing. It was the right thing to do so they could both focus—not blur the lines or cause any further confusion. However, the last few days they spent in Cambodia were his least favorite, if it was even right for him to personalize them. Ava had been cordial. No additional conversation than what needed to happen—none of her light banter. If it wasn't related to his duty to protect her, she didn't talk much to him. And although this was as things should have been from the beginning, he wasn't a fan of how things were going between them.

But this is what you wanted and suggested.

Even now, Ava kept to herself on the plane ride returning home. Whereas she used his shoulder as a pillow on the flight to Cambodia, they were on the second leg of this flight, and she used her neck pillow to sleep. And he knew it was uncomfortable because she joked about it, but that didn't keep her from using it anyway. Several times he wanted to ease her discomfort and gently adjust her so that her head rested on his shoulder, but that was crossing the line. Again. Exactly what they agreed neither of them would do.

Zack gave his attention to the files on his laptop screen. The man at the hospital hadn't been identified. Was he also the one who sent the letters and e-mail to Lamont? Whoever sent that message to Lamont's personal e-mail used a vanishing vpn. His firm could still trace it, but the process would take longer. Both loose ends he needed to tie ASAP.

Rick Fuller. Zack couldn't tie any of the recent events to him. In fact, he was in the office with Crystal when Ava was poisoned. Unless he hired someone to plant the poison, then it wouldn't make sense for Rick to be a suspect. Besides, the man wanted to be CEO, so poisoning Ava just didn't seem like something he'd do. And then there was the fact that someone got into her house without triggering the alarm. And the only way that would happen is if the person had a key. Rick wouldn't be that person. If Zack had to make a decision purely on instinct, Rick wouldn't be his guy.

And then there was Sharon Wertheimer. She was there when Ava was poisoned, but what motivation would she have? Couldn't be money. The woman and her family were loaded. Did she want Langston Brands for herself? Harming Ava wouldn't get that for her. It seemed more likely that the person would target Lamont, or even Crystal, with hopes that the rest of the family would be forced to sell the business. That seemed farfetched, and his instincts weren't leading him in that direction. Revenge? He found it hard to believe that Wertheimer would have a big enough issue with Ava to the point where she'd want to poison her. The woman didn't have any criminal history or associate with anyone who had a known criminal history. Looking at her just didn't feel right either.

He'd have to go in a different direction. Something he should have done before, but he'd look into past employees. Maybe he'd find something there. He had to because this situation had gone on far too long, and the longer it went unresolved, the greater danger Ava was in.

Zack sent an e-mail to Lamont requesting that he get a list of employees who'd left Langston Brands in the past five years. If the person behind the attacks on Ava was a past employee, it seemed unreasonable to think they would wait five years to act, but he had to cover his bases. A sense of peace settled over him when he hit send on the e-mail. He could feel it in his bones—this path would get him answers.

It had to.

Because the woman sleeping in the seat next to him was worth him exhausting every option until he uncovered the truth.

Chapter Seventeen

Ava slept on and off for an entire day once she arrived
back to The Four Kings' private facility to make up
for the terrible sleep she'd gotten on the plane, plus jet lag. How did
anyone ever get decent rest mid-air and not get a crook in their neck?

After showering and dressing in lounge clothes, she called
her big sister and boss, Crystal. The last time Ava communicated
with Crystal, Crystal confirmed that the bank preapproved the loan,
and as a result Crystal authorized Langston Brands to move forward
with the purchase of the new real estate in Phnom Penh. Ava never
had any doubt about that coming together. But with Rick gone, there
was a gap that needed to be filled.

Ava texted her.

A: Give me a call when you have a few minutes.

Crystal seemed to always be in the meeting, on a conference
call, or squeezing in time with Marcel. Ava suspected that he'd be
proposing soon with things falling into place for him. He'd secured
the district attorney seat and reconnected with the love of his life.
Quite naturally, he would be ready to marry her. Knowing him, he'd

probably already bought the ring—or at least had his eye on the perfect stone.

Crystal responded with a phone call.

"Hey, sis. Back and ready to work, I see. How are you?"

"I'm good. I think I've had enough rest for you and me, and I'm feeling a little antsy. I need to get out of this building."

"Have you talked this over with Zack? We can't have you prancing around these streets with that weirdo still out there."

"Well, we already know what he's going to say. 'What time do we need to leave?'" Ava said with her best Zack impression. She couldn't go outside the apartment without him. Well, Jax could escort her, but Zack normally personally saw to her safety.

Crystal chuckled. "It'll all be over soon. It has to be."

"Yeah." A beat of silence passed between them before Ava continued. "Now that Rick's gone, do you have anyone in mind to replace him?"

"No, not yet. I haven't thought about it much. Besides, it's only been a few days."

"And speaking of which, you never told me how the conversation went. I wish I could have been in the room."

"You know Rick, so I'm sure you can imagine him saying that every decision he made was for the betterment of the company and to save us money. He called it being efficient and effective, citing how production ticked up, which enabled us to sell more products and get them into stores faster. *Tuh!* Of all people, he was the last person I'd suspect to do something like this, especially considering how badly he wanted my job."

Ava cosigned, "Right. I'm sure in his mind, the sweatshops made sense."

Crystal *tsk*ed. Ava imagined the scowl her sister wore on the opposite phone line. "But Rick also knows operating in those conditions is contrary to what our company stands for."

Ava wasn't sure why, but Elaine Waters, had been on her mind since she arrived back in the States, and she wanted to suggest Crystal ask her to come back to Langston Brands to take Rick's place. That had to be why she'd been on her mind. Elaine had worked for Langston Brands for twenty years before leaving to work for a competitor, which surprised all of them when she left. Because she'd worked with them for so long, she'd been like family. So much so that they often referred to her as Auntie Elaine.

"Crys, what do you think of Elaine coming back to Langston Brands as Rick's replacement?"

"I don't know. I only know her personally since she left before I joined the company. I take it you have some thoughts about her, so let me hear them."

"She's been on my mind since I've been back in the States. I worked with her until she left the company. Actually, she trained me, so I can vouch for her. I'm fairly certain the main reason she left is because our competitor offered her a bigger salary with the title to match. Here, she was marketing director, but she wanted to be VP of marketing and sales."

"Which is your job."

"Right."

"If she's as good as you say she is, why didn't we try to compete with the offer?" Crystal asked.

"That's a question you'll have to ask Dad. Back then, he made the decisions."

"*Hmmm.* Since she's been on your mind, would you like to call her up to feel her out—see if she's even interested in coming back?"

"I'll reach out to her today and get back with you. Thanks for considering my suggestion."

"Of course. Even though I'm CEO, we're still a team. I couldn't run this company without my family."

"Thanks for saying that. I'll give you a call later." A warm feeling washed over Ava. She couldn't recall the last time her opinions were valued or when it felt like she was making a difference at Langston Brands.

Finally.

When Ava ended the call, she brewed a cup of coffee in her single-serve coffee maker, and doctored up the drink with cream and sugar. Blowing the hot liquid to cool it down so that she could take her first sip, she scrolled through her contacts until she came to Elaine's name. But she hesitated before calling.

Would Elaine think it weird for her to call after all this time? Sure, she ran into her at the restaurant a while back with promises to reach out, but Elaine was the farthest person from her mind with everything happening. She hadn't talked to her since she left Langston Brands, and Ava wasn't sure if her parents or Layla had either. There was only one way to find out. Ava hit the call button and held her breath. She shouldn't be so nervous based on Elaine's reaction when they ran into each other outside of the restaurant and considering they were once like family.

"Ava, is that you?" Elaine asked when she answered.

Ava perched on the arm of the sofa. "Hi, Aunt Elaine. It is me. How are you?"

"It's so wonderful to hear your voice. I'm doing great. How are you, my dear?"

"I'm doing well myself. Just returned from Cambodia."

"Sounds exotic. How about we catch up over coffee some time? I'd love to see you. It's been so long, and we never got together for that lunch like we said when we ran into each other last."

Ava took a sip of her own coffee and imagined the smile covering Elaine's face. Her wide eyes and dimples. She probably had a few more grays in her pixie cut now. Elaine was the person who inspired Ava to go with the shorter hairstyle before she let her hair grow back to its normal shoulder length.

It would be great to see Elaine again. Give her a bear hug. Look her in the eyes to gauge her sincerity when asking her if she wanted to return to Langston Brands. And if nothing else, just laying eyes on her would be nice considering Ava had nearly lost her life. She didn't want to take any relationships for granted.

But how would she see Elaine with Zack or Jax hovering over her? She didn't want anyone to know what was going on. Would it be wise to invite her over? Go over to her place? Zack or Jax could sit across the street and keep watch.

Ava placed her mug on the end table and held prayer hands to her chest. "I like that idea. Can we meet this afternoon or maybe tomorrow some time?" She held her breath.

"I'm free as a bird this week, taking some much-needed time off from work, so whatever suits you."

"I can meet you in a couple of hours." Ava's response erupted out of her like a mouth full of bubbles. Did she sound desperate? At least it didn't seem like Elaine held a grudge against her or her family. She sounded genuinely excited about talking to her.

"I can prepare my famous teacakes while we sit and chat over coffee. How does noon work for you?" Elaine asked.

"That sounds so good. I've missed your teacakes. Are you still at the same address?" Ava's stomach twinged at the fact she even had to ask.

"Sure am. See you soon."

"Soon."

Ava scrolled through her contacts. Now all she had to do was make arrangements with her bodyguard.

∞

Zack hadn't heard much from Ava since they'd returned, only that she was doing fine and getting some much-needed rest.

Janine, his cousin and The Four Kings' office assistant, saw to it that her refrigerator and pantry had been restocked with her staple items before they arrived. With Jax keeping watch outside of her door and the fully functioning alarm system, Zack didn't have any reasons to be concerned, which also allowed him to focus more on the work in front of him— Langston Brands' former employee list. For each employee who left over the last five years, Zack secured their personal information, reasons for leaving, current financial situation, known associates, criminal history, and where they were currently employed. Sifting through the information, Zack's intuition told him he was now on the correct path.

The first step in his analysis was to take a deep dive into the information of the highest ranking former employees. In his experience, executives didn't leave unless they were fatigued, fired, found a better opportunity, or felt unsupported. The first two people on his list were Miriam Becker and Elaine Waters. Miriam was finance director, and Elaine was marketing director prior to separating from the company. They were both now high-ranking executives at their current employers, both competitors of Langston Brands. Their last-known phone numbers were in his file, so Zack ran a location analysis on both phones. That process would take a while because it wasn't as efficient as it would have been if he could get close to their phone and capture their data like he did with Philip, but it still worked.

Interrupting his process, his phone rang with the ringtone he'd assigned to Ava. He never wanted to miss her call in case something was wrong.

Zack leaped out of his seat, poised to get to Ava as quickly as he could if she needed him. "Everything okay?"

"Yes. All is well, but I need to leave in a little while. I'm having coffee with a former Langston Brands employee at noon, and before you say anything, Elaine was like an aunt to me. It's completely safe to visit her at her house."

Zack peered back at his laptop screen. "What's Elaine's last name?"

"Waters. Why? Is there something wrong?"

"Mind telling me how this coffee date came about?"

Zack could hear Ava's soft huff through the line, though she tried to mask it. At this point, she knew the drill, but that didn't mean she had to like it. Lucky for him, whether she liked it or not didn't bother him. He'd told her he cared more about her safety than anything else so many times that she probably heard it in her sleep. So instead of addressing her mini tantrum, he waited until she gave an explanation.

Silence passed through the line for much longer than he liked.

"I called her. We're interested in seeing if she'd like to come back and take Rick's place," Ava said in an if-you-must-know tone.

"And why'd she leave before?"

"She wanted the vice president of marketing and sales seat, but she knew all along that the position would be mine and that my father's plan was for me and my sisters to run the company. Aunt Elaine understood that. However, when an opportunity for her to leave presented itself, she left. It was business, so we all still have love for her. Why is this relevant?"

Zack didn't want to get into another non-couple fight with Ava, so he chose his words carefully. "I'm looking into former Langston Brands employees. There's a good chance that whoever is behind the threats on your life could've once been on your payroll."

Ava released a heavy breath. "I can't tell you how to run your investigation, but if Aunt Elaine is on your list, you can scratch her off. I've known her forever. Like I said, she's practically family."

"Thanks for that insight." Based on what Ava shared, Elaine moved up on his list. Because of Ava's affection for the woman, he hoped she wasn't the one to blame. However, someone who knew her personally—and in his mind, had motive—was the ultimate suspect. But he wouldn't say that to Ava.

"You're welcome...And there's just one more thing: I'd like to go alone. It may not be a good look for me to go with a bodyguard. I know if I were her, I wouldn't want to go work anywhere where the executives were being poisoned and receiving threats."

"I hear you, but you should know me well enough by now to know that I'm not letting you go alone. I'll sit in the car nearby once I see that you're safely inside, but going alone is not an option."

"I'll take that."

"I know you're convinced that Elaine has nothing to do with this, but I need to be convinced, too. I need you to wear an earpiece that will allow me to listen in on your conversation."

"Are you kidding me?"

Zack opened his desk drawer and removed the small box, rolling it between his fingers. "It's pretty much invisible. She won't see it or even know it's there. Just act normal."

"I don't know, Zack. This makes me nervous."

"The way I see it, you have two choices: I come inside with you—you can tell her we're dating or whatever you need to say to make you feel comfortable—or you can wear the earpiece."

"We wouldn't want to blur any lines," Ava said, her tone holding a bit of sass, "so I guess I have no choice but to take the spy gear. Do I get a leather jacket, too?"

Zack chuckled. He'd almost said something that could be perceived as personal, but remembering their agreement back in Cambodia, he clamped his lips shut and took a breath before responding. "I'll see you in an hour to get you set up."

Chapter Eighteen

Had she fallen asleep and awakened in an episode of one of her favorite TV crime dramas? Because that's exactly how she felt slowing her car to a stop in front of Elaine's house with an earpiece communication device in her ear. Spy gear. Music often consoled her, induced nostalgia, and transported her mind back to happier times. On the drive over, she listened to R&B and hip-hop music from the nineties and early two thousands. Her favorite satellite radio station seemed to always know what she needed to hear, except when a Brian McKnight love song came across the airwaves. Under different circumstances, she would sing to the top of her lungs, but that wouldn't be appropriate knowing that Zack was listening to everything. What would it look like if she started singing about how she never felt this way about loving and how it never felt so good? The very definition of awkward.

Ava shifted her car into park and slowly filled her lungs with as much oxygen as they could withstand.

"Calm down, Ava. Be yourself, and forget I'm even here."

"Easy for you to say. You're trained to do this sort of thing, not me," she whispered, unsure of why considering she was alone in the car.

She reached for the door handle, and her heart slammed in her rib cage. Ava pressed her palm to her chest to force a steady rhythm. *This is crazy. And it's all Zack's fault.* She'd never consider or believe Elaine would be behind anything like this. Zack's suspicions were playing with her head.

The only way to address the jitters was to power through them and do what she came here to do—see her auntie and leave with high hopes of her rejoining the Langston Brands team.

Ava climbed out of her car and looked over her shoulder for Zack. She didn't think anything would happen, but having him near gave her comfort. However, with the quick cursory glance, she didn't spot his vehicle. Dang it. He was good. But where was he? She fought the urge to check for him again. He could hear everything, so that tidbit alone made up for the fact she couldn't see him.

Bushels of Knockout roses were lined in front of her porch. With freshly manicured grass and the white porch swing in front, the view looked like something she'd see in a *Better Homes & Gardens* magazine. In fact, Elaine probably deserved an article if one considered her famous teacakes in conjunction with her landscaping. Ava strolled along the cement path to the one-story red brick home until she stood next to the porch swing. Today would be like old times.

Ava raised her hand to ring the doorbell, but the door swung open before she could press the button.

"Come on in here, beautiful!" Elaine threw her arms around Ava's neck and squeezed. "It's so good to see you again." She released Ava and held her at arm's length, giving her a full body assessment. "Still gorgeous. I bet you're still sticking with that five in the morning gym routine, huh?"

Ava blushed. "Something like that."

"I bet you are. You're a stickler for routines and schedules. Come on in. The teacakes are ready, and the coffee is piping hot."

Ava followed Elaine into the residence. Lavender had been Elaine's home signature fragrance, but today it was coupled with fresh coffee beans.

"It smells so good in here. I think the last time I had teacakes is probably when I last visited you." That was probably five years ago, if not longer.

"Then I'd say it's been far too long." Elaine reached for Ava's purse. "I'll put this away for you in the hall closet. You can have a seat in the kitchen. The table is already set."

Ava handed Elaine her Langston Brands tote bag. While Elaine whisked out of the room to put her purse away, Ava followed her nose into the kitchen. Elaine's breakfast table for two near the bay window was set with a silver tray of teacakes, two novelty mugs, and a carafe of coffee. Ava stepped onto a barstool and took the seat facing the window. Outside the window were red and yellow flowers. Since Ava wasn't a flower person, she didn't know the types, only that they were beautiful and created a nice ambience. She could sit there and sip her coffee every morning while reading her daily devotional.

The rest of the kitchen was a chef's dream. A large, oversized island occupied the center. Stainless-steel appliances looked unused. Marble countertops. White cabinetry. That was a daredevil move, but something Elaine could get away with since she lived alone.

Elaine sauntered into the kitchen in a red maxi dress with pockets and her hair styled in a pixie cut with auburn highlights Ava hadn't noticed before now. She looked refreshed and younger than Ava remembered. Time was not her enemy.

"I hope I didn't keep you waiting for too long." Elaine waved her hand across the table game show—model style before taking her seat. "I baked all your favorites. Lemon. Caramel. Vanilla."

Ava inhaled and smiled. "I know. They smell delicious, and I'm happy you remembered."

Elaine reached across the table and took one of Ava's hands into her own. "Let's just address the elephant in the room so we can have a good time catching up."

Ava stiffened in her seat and locked eyes with Elaine.

"There are no hard feelings. I know you have a life, and keeping in touch works both ways. Your eyes hold a lot of guilt. In this moment, I want you to let it go. There's no love lost over me leaving Langston Brands to work with Boutique Beauty Brands."

Ava squeezed Elaine's hand. "You have no idea how happy I am to hear you say that. Thanks, Aunt Elaine."

Elaine offered a comforting motherly smile before switching into that old familiar girlfriend-like mode. "So, spill the tea. What have I missed? Please tell me that none of you have gotten married." She poured a cup of coffee for her and Ava and settled back into her seat.

Ava doctored up her coffee with vanilla caramel creamer and one packet of sugar substitute and chuckled. "You haven't missed that much, although Crystal may be closer to getting down the aisle again."

"Really?"

"Yes, ma'am. Marcel Singleton."

Elaine slapped her knee. "That's right. The DA. He's made it no secret how much he adores her. How did that slip my mind?"

"I don't know. It's kind of hard to miss. She supports him at every political event. I'm sure the whole city knows they're a thing by now." Ava stopped short of bringing up the murder situation where Marcel represented Crystal. No need to relive that nightmare, especially considering their plan to ask her to come back and work with them at Langston Brands.

"Chalk it up to old age. And my dear Layla? How is she?"

"Layla is Layla. Feisty as ever. It's going to take a strong man to love her and not run away licking his wounds because she hurt his feelings."

Elaine chuckled. "And you've always fallen somewhere in between both of your sisters. How are things for you? Work, love life? I want to hear everything. It's been so long."

Ava saw a genuine concern in Elaine's eyes, yet because Elaine worked for a competitor, there wasn't a lot she could say to her. Unfortunately, their conversations regarding work had to be surface level. Ava removed one of each flavor teacakes and placed them on the saucer in front of her.

"Not much is going on with me. Well, I take that back. I just came back from Cambodia. Mostly a work trip where I helped to find a new location for our manufacturing operations."

Elaine picked up a lemon teacake and took a bite. She frowned as she chewed. "You mean to tell me that Lamont allowed you to do that? Isn't Crystal CEO?"

"She is, but she's been so busy lately that I went in her place."

"This is just between me and you, but I'm glad they're finally giving you an opportunity to shine."

Ava's face must have been distorted because Elaine tried to fix her statement.

"Now, don't get me wrong. Your position as vice president of marketing and sales is important, and so is being on the board, but you've always been outshined by Crystal because she's the oldest and Layla because she's the youngest. It seems Lamont is finally seeing you."

Perhaps the way she felt about being stuck in the middle all these years wasn't in her head; however, she wasn't there to have this conversation with Elaine. And she put on her best smile in hopes to show Elaine she wasn't fazed by what she'd said.

"Seems that way," Ava answered.

"Well, I'm glad." Elaine tapped her hand and leaned forward in her seat like she was preparing to hear juicy details. "Now, tell me about your love life. You're a gorgeous young woman—the total package. I know there must be someone."

Her stomach compressed like grapes in a winepress. Not because of the question about her love life, but because for the first time since being inside, she remembered that Zack was listening to everything she said. If he hadn't been, maybe she would have asked Elaine for some advice just to ensure she wasn't crazy. But she had to tread carefully. Technically, they weren't in a relationship, but she couldn't say she wasn't interested in anyone. Shoot, the confusion surfaced all over again.

"Well," Ava sang and bit into a teacake, "it's complicated."

"See, that's this new-age stuff. Back in my day, it was either you liked the man or you didn't. You were together or you weren't. There was no in between. So, this complicated situation…is he married?"

"No," Ava near shouted.

Elaine gripped her chest, inhaled, and then raised a hand toward heaven. "Oh, thank God."

"I think you know me better than that."

"*Whew*, and I'm glad about it. You don't want those troubles. Want to share what makes it complicated?"

"Right guy. Wrong time." That comment slipped out, and she wished she could take it back. Maybe Zack wasn't quite listening because this line of talk was boring. The chances of that were skinnier than her tightest pair of skinny jeans. The man didn't miss anything.

Elaine lifted her coffee mug in salute. "Oh, honey, every woman has been there. You're still young, so I hope it works out better for you than it did for me."

Ava detected a hint of sadness in Elaine's voice that a part of her wanted to explore. Was that the reason Elaine never married?

"Speaking as a woman with experience, got any advice for me?" Ava asked and took another bite of her teacake.

Elaine sipped her coffee and stared in Ava's direction as if she were recalling a memory. Her gaze distant. The longing in her eyes evident. "If you love him, tell him. Don't make the mistake of believing in fairytales and thinking it'll all work itself out in this neat little bow. Face your fears and your feelings. Oh, and think big picture. We put emphasis on so many petty things that don't matter—things that are temporary. Simply go for it because tomorrow isn't promised."

And just when Ava thought Elaine finished her advice, she added, "Our biggest regrets in life are not the things we did and said, but the actions we didn't take and the words we didn't say. Get what I'm saying?"

Ava sipped her coffee and nodded, allowing Elaine's words to sink in.

"You could very well not be here tomorrow, and then you've potentially missed out on love because of something silly like work."

∞

Zack's ears perked up.

Before now, the conversation between Ava and Elaine didn't warrant any concern. He'd driven past Elaine's house twice now and parked a safe distance away to where he could still see the front door. With his laptop planted on the center console, he focused his attention on the files he had on both Miriam Becker and Elaine Waters. He started his review on Miriam before he met with Ava to take this drive over to Elaine's house. Couple what he reviewed then to what he looked at now, and nothing in her file caused him any concern. She left Langston Brands to work at a competitor, who at this point wasn't much of a direct competitor. Langston Brands' sales put them in a different tax bracket. Miriam had no connection to Ava since starting at the smaller company. Her finances were in order. No debt. No investments either. And she wasn't in the state the night Ava was poisoned. Known associates weren't connected to Ava in any way, nor where they in town the night of Ava's poisoning. Her IP address also didn't match the address from where Lamont received the email. And it was unlikely that she'd have access to Ava's house. Miriam didn't fit the profile of the person they were looking for. Plus, his instincts were cold when it came to her.

And then there was Elaine.

He'd been combing through her file, but mostly listening to the conversation between her and Ava. Elaine appeared to have genuine affection toward Ava, which would be a cue for him to automatically scratch her off the list. However, he'd worked enough criminal cases both on and off the force to know that many crimes were committed by those who had a close relationship to the victim. And quite honestly, that was one of the things that made him more suspicious of her...the way Ava talked about how much she considered Elaine to be family. Ava may have believed she was convincing him of Elaine's lack of involvement, when all she did was help move Elaine to the top of his list.

Zack huffed. Complicated? Was that how Ava saw him and their involvement?

He wouldn't quite describe them that way. More like on pause so they could focus on her safety, yet they also didn't agree on how they'd move forward once he was no longer her bodyguard. And the truth was he didn't know. He should be ready to move on since Mariah had been gone for nearly five years, but could he?

Zack's thoughts settled on Elaine's last statement. *Missing out on love because of something silly like work.* Ava never mentioned anything about work being the reason things were complicated between them.

Instead of verbally responding to Elaine's comment, Ava coughed like she was gasping for air. Blood swooshed through his veins to his fingertips. "Ava, say something right now to let me know you're okay, or I'm coming in."

Ava coughed and gasped again.

"Oh, you don't still have a tree nut allergy, do you? That must have slipped my mind. I was out of white flour, so I substituted almond flour instead. That doesn't bother you, does it?" Although the way Elaine said it didn't lead Zack to believe she was sorry about the mishap at all. In fact, it was very much intentional if he had to guess.

"My…purse," Ava said through chopped breaths.

"Ava? I'm on my way."

"O–kay," she said through another gasp for air.

Zack started the engine with the push of a button, his tires left skid marks as he raced down the street.

He heard what sounded like fumbling and clanking dishes. "Darn it. Do you need your purse? Is your EpiPen in there? Let me go grab that for you," Elaine said without a shred of urgency in her voice.

Zack could hear her footsteps trailing away. However, it seemed she turned around. "But before I go, let me just say that I'm glad that poisoning you at the restaurant didn't work or that we couldn't get the ethylene glycol into your system at the hospital because it really was great to see you again."

He threw his car into park and raced up the path to Elaine's door.

"But why?" Ava's voice was faint between gasps for air, but he understood her.

"Oh, this is payback for your mother taking Lamont away from me, for you taking my job as VP of marketing and sales, and for Langston Brands taking BBB's shelf space with Wertheimer and Fitzgerald. Honey, this has been a long time coming."

Zack was prepared to kick the door down, but the front door opened when he twisted the knob. Not knowing or even caring if Elaine had a weapon, he raced through the living room into the open concept kitchen to find Elaine standing over Ava's limp body. Aside from the tiny bumps covering her skin, the image of her body on the kitchen floor reminded him of when they first met.

Chapter Nineteen

"Who are you, and how'd you get in my house?" Elaine shrieked. She snatched the fireplace poker out of its holder, and mid-swing, Zack whipped his weapon from his holster.

"I wouldn't do that if I were you."

Zack gave her a quick assessment. Elaine was the type who thought she'd be able to move faster than him because of her small frame. And sure enough, she charged at him and swung the fireplace poker. Zack caught the stick and plucked it from her grasp. Elaine stumbled away from him until her backside was up against the wall. Her chest heaved up and down while fiery darts shot from her squinted eyes.

"What did you do to her?"

Knowing the answer before Elaine responded, Zack knelt at Ava's side and jammed an EpiPen into her thigh. She'd given it to him when he moved her into the Four Kings' private facility. Just in case. He'd carried that thing around in his jacket like it was his own lifeline. And to think she didn't believe he'd ever have to use it.

213

Several seconds later, she gasped, and her body came to life in his arms. Her eyes fluttered open.

"Ava, are you okay? We've got to get you to the hospital."

She scratched her arms. "I think I'll be okay."

Zack shook his head. "I'm not taking any chances."

"Aunt Elaine, how could you?"

"Stop whining. That's always been your problem. You whine too much. I've about had it with you and your family thinking you can just walk all over me and not face the consequences of your actions. Your father. Your mother. And you."

Ava's wide eyes and mouth fueled Elaine's anger.

"Oh, so your father never told you how he led me on? Led me to believe that he'd leave Dana for me. Led me to believe that I'd someday run the company with him. Oversee marketing and sales. That's right, you're in the wrong seat." By this time, the woman was crying and shouting. "My seat. I trained you, and you took my job. And did you all think I was just going to sit around while you took the biggest break of my career? I thought for sure Crystal's murder case would take Langston Brands down and I could just sit back and watch while the company burned to the ground. But when Wertheimer told me she planned to put your bags in the stores instead of ours, I knew it was time to act. I thought for sure getting my nephew to poison you and telling Wertheimer about the sweatshops would do the trick."

Elaine bowed.

Ava scrunched her eyebrows. "And the letters. Was that you, too?"

Elaine released an unsettling chuckle. The woman was unstable. "Brilliant, wasn't it? You all are creatures of habit. It wasn't hard to get the letters to you. I knew when Lamont checked his mail. Same time every day at a quarter till noon. And you? You go to the gym every Monday, Wednesday, and Friday at five in the morning. Kickboxing on Saturdays with your sisters. I did think it would be difficult to get that last letter to you, but surprisingly, my key still works."

Zack made a mental note to change the locks on Ava's doors.

"My plan was almost perfect, except I didn't expect Lamont to hire this private security firm. He—" she pointed at Zack— "made it hard to get to you, even in the hospital when my nephew tried to finish you off." A sinister glimmer lit her eyes. "But when you called me to have coffee, you made my job a little easier."

Ava shook her head, blinking as if she were trying to relieve the fuzziness in her eyes. "I just can't believe this. You were like family."

Elaine scoffed. "If I was like family, y'all would've never treated me the way you did. I haven't heard from any of you until you called me today. Is that how you treat family?"

Zeke rushed through the door with two cops following.

"Elaine Waters," one of the cops said, "you're under arrest for four counts of attempted murder. Place your hands behind your back." He cuffed her and said, "You have the right to remain silent.

Anything you say can and will be used against you in a court of law. You have the right to an attorney. If you cannot afford an attorney, one will be appointed to you."

"Oh, don't worry, I can afford an attorney, and I'll spend every dime I have to take down Lamont's low-down, dirty behind," Elaine screamed and bucked under the police officers' hold as they escorted her out of the house.

Zack lifted Ava to a standing position. Evidence of the allergic reaction was more prominent on her cheeks. The tiny puffy bumps on her skin were disappearing, but some of the redness remained. "You look better, but I will feel more comfortable if you saw a doctor."

"I'm okay, but it couldn't hurt." She turned to Zeke. "How'd you get here so fast?"

Zeke removed the small earpiece from his ear. "I was listening, too, and not far away in case Zack needed backup. Your voice became faint. I could hear you gasping. And Zack had already communicated his suspicions. When he asked you to confirm you were okay, you didn't. That was our cue to act."

"I am so grateful to you all. I guess you were right about Elaine."

The light in Ava's eyes dimmed. He wasn't the type of person who needed to be right, and this was one situation where he wished he'd been wrong.

"I'm sorry, Ava." Instinctively, he brushed her bangs to the side of her face, smoothing his thumb along her forehead.

"Once again, I owe you my life."

"You don't owe me anything. I was just—"

"Doing your job," Ava finished his sentence.

He'd come to understand that she didn't care much for him saying that, although it was true. On every occasion, she squinted before rolling her eyes. What else was he supposed to say? Surely by this point, the two of them should have an understanding.

Zeke looked between the two of them. "Is there something going on that I don't know about. What's up with you two?"

Zack kept his eyes locked on Ava, scooped her up in his arms, and carried her out the door. "It's complicated."

∞

It didn't have to be complicated.

Zack made it that way. Like now. She was perfectly capable of walking, yet he carried her out of the house. And she wasn't complaining because she hadn't been carried by any man before now, and she loved how it felt to be protected by him and wrapped in his arms. Yet, he used his job as a crutch. Was it his job to protect her? Yes. But he wasn't supposed to make her feel like he cared about her beyond his paid duties.

The good news about this complication was that it was now over. Case solved. Crystal fired Rick. Elaine was on her way to jail.

Zack opened the passenger-side door to his truck and slid Ava onto the seat.

"Wait," she said before he closed the door. "My car is here. I can drive myself. I'm fine."

Zack positioned himself between her and the door, with one hand resting on the hood and the other on the door. He peered down at her, and for the first time, she saw something different in his eyes, but couldn't name it. "Zeke will arrange for Jax to come get your car and take it back to The Four Kings' private facility. I'm driving you to the hospital to get you checked out, so let's not waste time."

As if that settled it, Ava shifted in the seat and secured her seatbelt. Zack rounded the truck, climbed in, and searched for the nearest hospital using his phone's map service. Selecting the address, he set the radio to the satellite R&B station she liked, and drove away in silence.

Ava had to wonder what was going through his head, but she'd scream if he used the words *I'm just doing my job* again. To combat that response before he could even give it, she said, "I think you've done your job, Zack. And you've done it well. You don't have to babysit me anymore."

He glanced in her direction for all of two seconds before redirecting his attention to the road. Zack crinkled his brow, and his chest jerked in a huff, but he remained silent.

Ava turned off the radio and planted her hands in her lap. "I'm serious. This is going beyond your contractual obligation to me and my father, not to mention adding to the element of confusion. Why are you doing this?"

Silenced hinged between them.

"For a few minutes today, I experienced fear—fear that I'd lose you. When I asked if you were okay, a part of me relived

Mariah's death when you didn't answer. I can't lose you, too, Ava. And if something had happened to you, this time it would've been my fault."

"Zack—"

"I hear you, and I understand you feel okay, but I need to hear the doctor say it. Can you do that for me?"

If he was asking like that, she'd do anything for him. Why did his voice have to make her melt? This was supposed to be the point where they said good-bye.

Ava nodded. "Yes, I can." What else was she supposed to say to a request like that anyway?

His strong jawline flexed, and she'd come to learn that when he did that, he was about to say something important. She shifted in her seat to face him, the seatbelt now awkward, but she didn't care.

He glanced at her once more then covered her hands with one of his. His warm hand squeezed hers. "I care about you, Ava, and it's not my intention to confuse you or make this situation complicated. And to be clear, I'm not talking about my duty to protect you because Lamont hired me. I care way beyond that."

Zack slowed his truck to a stop in a parking space inside the hospital parking garage. He turned to face her. The intensity and warmth of his eyes made her heart drum a hundred different ways. Couple the way he looked at her with his confession of feelings, and Ava's skin warmed from head to toe. Thankfully, the heat had nothing to do with the allergic reaction to the almond flour she'd had earlier. But it was all because the mere idea of being near this man did funny things to her. And she liked it.

"I care about you, too. So, what are we going to do about all this caring?" Ava half-teased.

"We're going to find a way to make it work."

Twenty

Ava had spent the last two weeks adjusting to life as it was pre-poisoning and pre-Zack. It was weird not having him around all the time. Funny, because while in the midst of her ordeal, all she wanted was her freedom, but now she couldn't wait to see him again. After the doctor issued her a clean bill of health, Zack was satisfied. He dropped her off at The Four Kings' private facility where she spent her final night.

Her mother and father arrived back in the states three days after that ordeal, and she still hadn't had the conversation she wanted to have with them. The conversation that needed to be had about Elaine. Ava had fifty questions, beginning with whether her father had really been involved in a relationship with Elaine. Did her mother know? Was that the real reason why Elaine left Langston Brands?

She had two big meetings today—her family meeting to get this Elaine business out in the open, and then there was Sharon Wertheimer. Ava prayed this deal could go through. It was about time their family and Langston Brands had a win.

Ava slowed her car to a stop in her parents' semi-circle driveway. She'd grown up in the red-and-brown brick two-story, five-bedroom home. She strolled through the French doors through the foyer. Hard conversations were always held in the kitchen over a large meal. And today wasn't any different. The aroma of Cornish hens, her mother's butter dinner rolls, broccoli cheese casserole, mustard greens, and sweet potatoes called to her. And yes, she could identify the smell of each dish. Probably because she was hungry.

Crystal, Layla, and her parents were already seated around the table in the same order they'd always sat. Her father at the head of the table. Her mother to his right with Layla next to her. Crystal to his left. Ava's spot was next to her.

"Hi everyone," she said through her biggest smile, which hid her nervousness. Nervous because she was afraid of what she might learn—that Elaine may have been telling the truth. And if so, how could her father betray her mother and their family that way?

"Hey, Ava," they all sang in unison.

Ava took her seat next to Crystal and whispered, "What did I miss?"

"Nothing. We've been waiting for you."

"You had like two more seconds, and I was going to suggest we start eating without you. I'm starving. Come on, Dad. Let's pray," Layla added.

The group chuckled.

"Father God, thanks for bringing us together once again. Thank You for Your grace and mercy and this food before us. Guide us in Your truth and walk with us. In Jesus' name. Amen."

"Amen," the rest of the group said.

"Alright, Lay, you can fill your belly," Ava said.

"You don't have to tell me twice," she said and reached for the pan of Cornish hens, served herself, and passed it to her mother.

They spent several minutes chatting about updates in Cambodia regarding the new building. The transaction would close in two weeks, and after moving the equipment, they could get their people back to work. In addition, Crystal had appointed a member of her team to provide oversight of their overseas operations until they could replace Rick, so thankfully, the sweatshop issue was resolved. That was solid news Ava could give to Wertheimer, with hopes of moving forward with her proposed deal.

"I'm glad we were able to fix the sweatshop situation. And I guess if it weren't for Elaine, there's no telling how much longer Rick would've been able to keep this under the radar."

"I take full responsibility for his actions," her father said. "I trusted him too much and gave him too much power."

"You didn't make the decisions, Dad. Rick did," Ava said. "But there is something that's been bothering me about Elaine."

Before now, Ava had never mentioned Elaine alluded to a relationship with her father. Partly because she wasn't sure if she wanted to know the truth—a truth that could likely alter the way she saw her father and the esteemed pedestal she'd placed him on her entire life. And what if this was news to her mother? Although Elaine didn't make it sound that way. But after everything she'd done, Ava couldn't trust her. Her grandmother had a saying: Always get the truth from the horse's mouth.

Her father placed his utensils on his plate and gave her his full attention. He rested his hands on either side of his plate and looked her square in the eye. "What's that?"

Ava swallowed her anxiety and squared her shoulders, preparing for whatever truth he gave. "Aside from Elaine being upset about me being named VP of marketing and sales, she also mentioned that she was in a relationship with you, and you led her to believe that you would one day leave Mom and our family to be with her. Is that true?"

Ava held her breath.

Her father and mother shared a knowing look, the thing they did when they were having a silent conversation with their eyes that only the two of them could understand. Her mom took a deep breath and covered his hand, giving him the nod, which meant it was okay for him to say whatever he was about to say.

He cleared his throat. "Elaine and I never had an intimate relationship. One night while working late at the office, she kissed me." He paused and looked at his wife before returning his attention to Ava. "And to be forthcoming, I kissed her back. Nothing happened past that, and she and I talked about it and agreed nothing like that could ever happen again because I love my wife and my family, and I'd never do anything to jeopardize what we've built.

Elaine claimed to understand, but she continued making advances toward me."

Layla butted in, "And she's been all up in our house acting like she was family."

Their mother said, "And at one point she was. I loved Elaine like a sister—until she betrayed me. When she saw that Lamont was serious about keeping his vows and his family together, she decided she could no longer work with Langston Brands."

Her dad added, "That was the best move for her. Elaine was becoming delusional and obsessed. Showing up at our home uninvited. Sending topless pictures of herself to my phone and e-mail. If she hadn't made the decision to leave on her own, she would've been fired."

"Or cut," their mom added.

Ava and her sisters laughed.

"And to think we were considering bringing her back. Why didn't you two ever tell us any of this?" Crystal asked.

"She'd always been good to you girls, and we didn't want that to affect your relationship with her, but now I see that was a mistake. I never would've thought she'd try to hurt any of you," their mom said.

Ava's posture relaxed. She'd hoped what Elaine said wasn't true about her father, and now she could rest easy tonight.

When they finished dinner, her mom said, "Ava, why don't you come to the kitchen to help me with dessert?"

At thirty-nine years old, her mother had never asked her to do such a thing. Though a simple request, with heavy feet and tingles slithering down her spine, Ava trailed her into the kitchen.

Her mother placed the dishes in the dishwasher and turned to face Ava, her arms folded across her chest. "I was hoping we'd see Zack with you today."

Ava maneuvered around her and rinsed her own plate before adding it to the rack. "Why would you think that? I don't need his services anymore."

"Have you forgotten that I saw you two in Cambodia? That man would protect you for free."

Ava chuckled. "Things between us have gotten complicated. We just haven't figured them out yet."

"And just when do you plan to figure them out?"

As crazy as it sounded, and as much as she missed him, she hadn't seen him since she moved out of his company's private facility two weeks ago.

"Very soon. I'm leaving here to meet Ms. Wertheimer for coffee. I'll see him tonight or tomorrow."

Her mother held her chin and peered into her eyes. "What are you afraid of?"

Afraid that Zack isn't over his deceased wife.

Afraid that he still wasn't ready to move on.

"Nothing. We'll get it together."

"I've just never seen you light up the way you did when he was around. And I wanted to make sure you're okay. Didn't want to bring it up in front of your sisters in case you haven't shared with them yet."

Ava huffed. "It's okay. They have their own speculations, especially Layla."

"Maybe she's had a premonition or vision or whatever she likes to call them."

Ava chuckled. "Please don't get her started."

Her mom rubbed her back then grabbed the dessert. "Come on. Let's rejoin the family and enjoy this delicious chocolate cake."

Back inside the dining room, Ava reclaimed her seat. Looking around the table, her family's chatter filling the room, her world was right again, and her heart now full—well, almost. There was just one more thing she needed to do.

∞

"Come back down to earth," Zeke said.

"What do you mean? I'm here. I'm listening," Zack said.

Zack and his three brothers stood around the Kings table, which was their high-tech oversized computer, discussing the details of Zeke's current assignment, protecting a candidate campaigning for the Texas governor seat. The candidate's campaign manager, Olivia Singleton, received threats that if her candidate didn't back out of the race, he would meet his maker at the next campaign rally. Zeke already had a plan in place, but wanted to run it by his brothers for their input.

Zeke crossed his arms over his chest and cocked his head to the side. "Physically, yes, but mentally, you're not. I'm glad to have you back in the game, but I need your mind here, too, man. Let's keep it a buck for a minute. What's going on with you?"

Ava. All Ava. But his thoughts of her didn't prevent him from doing his job.

"Nothing. I'm all good, and I'm mentally here. You can keep going with the plan. I'm following."

"Nah, bro. Zeke is right," one of the twins, Josh, said. "Something is different about you. Since Jake and I have been out in the field, we haven't been around, so I can't pinpoint it."

"Yeah, so 'fess up so we can get back to work," Jake added.

"What is this, Attack Zack day?"

Zack rose to his full stature and eyed Zeke, daring him to say anything about Ava.

"You've been like this since the Langston assignment ended," Zeke said.

"Chill, Zeke. I'm good."

Zeke tossed his phone across the table to Zack. "But you can be better. Just call the woman, and get it over with."

Josh and Jake leaned away and looked Zack up and down wearing that same what-is-going-on face. Simultaneously, they asked, "What woman?"

Zack shook his head and tossed Zeke's phone back to him. "I can handle Ava, so just chill, and let's get back to work."

Because work was what kept him from focusing on her.

Work rescued him—both when he lost Mariah and when his protection detail ended for Ava.

He'd never been one to lack confidence, but he wasn't one hundred percent sure he was ready to open himself up to that vulnerability again.

You already have.

There was nothing else he could do with the emotions stirring inside of him about Ava, but give in to them. The sooner that happened, the better off he'd be, right?

Perhaps he needed more time.

Jake walked over and slapped him on the back. "Man, I'm happy for you. You deserve some happiness, and if Ava—that's her name, right?—does that for you, don't punish yourself."

"I think I may have said something to that effect, too," Zeke added and shared details about Zack carrying Ava out of Elaine's house when she was perfectly fine to walk.

"I'm not taking relationship advice from three single men."

Josh butted in, "But we aren't any old single men. We're the ones who have your back. And she's done something to you, so I say let her keep doing it."

Keep doing it? He could go for another kiss or the feel of her hand in his or her arms wrapped around his waist in a hug or the way she looked at him that made him feel like he could run through walls. None of that sounded like a bad idea.

"If I agree to take your advice under consideration, can we get back to work and focus on the task in front of us?"

"Absolutely," Jake said.

Zeke nodded. "That's all I'm asking."

"Yep," Josh answered.

"Then we have a deal."

He moreso made the deal with himself. He'd punished himself since she moved out of The Four Kings' private facility, giving her time to adjust—at least that was the lie he told himself. That ended today.

∞

Ava sat across the table from Sharon Wertheimer at a local coffee shop. When was the last time she enjoyed sipping coffee outside of her home or doing anything outside of her home for that matter without looking over her shoulder or having Zack do so on her behalf? It felt good to live normally again and slide back into her normal routine.

Ava sipped her vanilla latte. "Thanks for meeting with me, Ms. Wertheimer."

Ms. Wertheimer slid closer to the table and rested against it like Ava was one of her closest girlfriends and about to dish some juicy news. "You know I'll make time for you, Ava."

"We've taken the sweatshop allegations seriously and have made efforts to improve the situation. We can't have our company tied to any unfair labor practices." Ava shared the details of their new facility and how they fired the person responsible for the sweatshops in the first place.

"That is wonderful news. I had no doubt your team would take care of the situation. It was actually quite surprising when I heard about it, and it's unfortunate that my brother-in-law Rick had his hands in it. I'm quite disappointed in him. We all are."

"My father is, too, however, we wish him nothing but the best." Ava could've gone on and on about how great Rick was and how she was confident he'd learned his lesson and would do well in his next position somewhere else, but there was no need for that. Though she didn't wish him harm, he was not high up on her list of people she cared about.

Ms. Wertheimer waved her hand as if she was flicking a fly away. "Yeah, he's a grown man. He'll figure it out. But what I'm most excited about is this new partnership between Wertheimer and Langston Brands." She clasped her hands at her chest like a prissy cheerleader.

"Trust me. I think this is the best move for both of our companies."

Ms. Wertheimer sipped her cup of black coffee, whipped out her phone, and pecked away at the screen. "I'll have that contract sent over to your office by close of business Monday."

Ms. Wertheimer's words were like nineties R&B music to her ears. Comforting. Feel-good. Heart tingling.

"I look forward to it."

She'd accomplished what she set out to do—help get her family's company back on track. And Ava had put her confidence in this deal to help catapult them to where they needed to be. As much as she enjoyed chatting with Ms. Wertheimer about the newest fashion trends, Ava had one more thing she needed to settle.

When they finished their cups of coffee and bid their good-byes, Ava's phone rang.

Zack.

She hadn't been avoiding him, but more like giving him the time she thought he needed.

"Hey," she answered.

"Hey." The word dragged from his lips. "I know we agreed to meet later, but any chance you're available now?"

"I'm leaving the coffee shop on the main road outside of my neighborhood."

"Do you mind waiting? I can be there in about fifteen minutes."

Ava checked the time for no reason. The only other plan she had later that day was to connect with him.

"No. I don't mind. I'll grab a table and wait for you." Ava's heart inflated with anticipation as she stood in line and ordered another specialty coffee.

"Thanks. See you shortly."

It had to be unnatural for her to constantly swoon under the command of his voice, but she needed a clear mind, so she focused on the sounds of coffee shop music pouring from their sound system and her second latte sitting before her. She didn't like it when people changed meeting times at the last minute because in her world, that often meant something was wrong, so she rehearsed what she'd say to him.

It's okay. I understand. It was fun while it lasted. But that didn't sound right. That was more like what she'd hear on TV.

I care about you, too, but I understand your need to process.... Okay, that was even crazier.

Why was she thinking the worst?

"I'm clearly losing my mind. Maybe I have traces of almond hitched in my body, and it's causing a delayed reaction, making me go crazy," she said to her coffee cup.

Saving her from her crazy thoughts, Zack walked through the door. He looked even more handsome than he did the last time she saw him, strolling through the coffee shop in the made-for-him leather jacket. When he locked eyes with her, he didn't look away. He held her eyes, mind, and soul hostage. Her heart melted with each advancing step.

She stood to greet him, not realizing her lips were slightly parted until he took her into his arms and connected his lips with hers. In public. In front of every patron in the coffee shop. At that moment, her heart could've been identified as liquid gold. He'd turned her into mush. Again.

Breathless, he broke the kiss and gestured for her to sit while taking the seat next to her. "Ava, the last week has been torture for me. Not seeing you. Not hearing from you. I wanted to give you time to readjust, and to be transparent, time for myself to be sure my heart was ready to move on. To be yours. And it is. I want to be with you, Ava."

Zack wiped her cheeks with his thumbs. Goodness, she didn't even realize tears had spilled out of her eyes. Why was she so emotional?

"I've missed you as well. It's been hard for me, too. But I don't want you to see your dead wife when you look at me. I don't want you to be here for me because you feel like you couldn't be there for her. I want it to be me, Ava—" she pointed to her chest— "that you care about. I can't compete with a ghost, and I won't."

"You don't have to. All I want is you."

The intensity and sincerity in his eyes convinced her of his truth, and she wanted nothing more than to be with the man who made her heart sing.

"And me is everything you get."

It was Ava's turn to seal the deal with a kiss, connecting their souls once more. Who would've thought it had to take her going through a life-or-death situation to find the man of her dreams? And to think Elaine said she was in the wrong seat. If you asked her, she was exactly where she needed to be.

THE END

Dear reader,

What did you think of Ava and Zack? I love their story and for now, it is my favorite book. If you read, The Reunion, did you pick up on the subtle hints about what's coming next? You'll see Marcel's sister, Olivia Singleton, again. You'll also see more of the Kingsland brothers in their own series. You have to know I'm excited about that and I hope you are too.

But before we can get there, we have to close out this series with Layla's story. We'll see if those premonitions she's hinted at throughout The Reunion and The Wrong Seat have any merit. (wink, wink)

Please take a moment to let me know what you think by leaving a review on Amazon/Goodreads/Bookbub.

Until next time,

Natasha

About the Author

Natasha writes Christian fiction and devotionals. When she isn't reading or writing, she spends her time working out, swimming or watching movies with her family. She lives in the Houston metro area with her husband and three children.

Connect with Natasha online:

Bookbub @NatashaDFrazier

Instagram @author_natashafrazier

Twitter @author_natashaf

TikTok @author_natashafrazier

Facebook @craves.2012

Website: www.natashafrazier.com

Also by Natasha D. Frazier

Devotionals

The Life Your Spirit Craves

Not Without You

Not Without You Prayer Journal

The Life Your Spirit Craves for Mommies

Pursuit

Fiction

Love, Lies & Consequences

Through Thick & Thin: Love, Lies & Consequences Book 2

Shattered Vows: Love, Lies & Consequences Book 3

Out of the Shadows: Love, Lies & Consequences Book 4

Kairos: The Perfect Time for Love

Fate (The Perfect Time for Love series)

With Every Breath (The McCall Family Series, book 1)

With Every Step (The McCall Family Series, book 2)

With Every Moment (The McCall Family Series, book 3)

The Reunion (Langston Sisters, book1)

Non-Fiction

How Long Are You Going to Wait?